Ecstacy

Christie G. Douglas (signature)

Christie Douglas

Milligan Books   **California**

Published and Distributed by:
Milligan Books, Inc.
An imprint of Professional Business Consultants

Cover Design
Clint D. Johnson

Formatting
Alpha Desktop Publishing

First Printing, February 2003
10987654321

ISBN 0-9725941-4-0

Publisher's note

Milligan Books, Inc.
1425 W. Manchester Ave., Suite C
Los Angeles, California 90047
www.milliganbooks.com
(323) 750-3592

Nineteen Extraordinary Women who have inspired me to keep writing ...and to keep dreaming ...

- Betty H. Douglas (my Mom)
- Dr. Rosie Milligan
- Oprah Winfrey
- Toni Morrison
- Rev. Candace Cole
- Dr. Maya Angelou
- Evangeline Seward
- Patti Labelle
- Betty Griffin Keller
- Barbara Streisand
- Laura Young
- Halle Berry
- Dr. Hansonia Caldwell
- Whoopi Goldberg
- Ann Ehrenclou
- Barbara Walters
- Dr. Joyce Johnson
- Condoleezza Rice
- Dr. Sally Etcheto

Dedication

This is dedicated to the memory of my dear Aunties: Geraldine Williams, Gaynell Daughtrey, Margaret Blakeley, Bernice Williams, Othalia Douglas and Ricahrd Hinton.

To dream anything that you want to dream. That is the beauty of the human mind.

To do anything that you want to do. That is the strength of human will.

To trust yourself to test your limits. That is the courage to succeed.–Bernard Edmunds (American writer)

Acknowledgments

I would like to first acknowledge my Lord and Savior, Jesus Christ, for being my source and inspiration, and just for His enduring grace throughout this venture.

Special Thank you: Mom and Dad (Betty & William Douglas): I Love You So Much. Thank you for always supporting me, and never giving up on my dreams!

Thank You: my entire family & Friends: (especially)

Joanne & Dennis Austin, Tanya Norville, Joe & Ann Hinton & family, Patricia & Clifton Lewis, Ruby & John Davis, Patrick Deon Mayfield & family, Carol White & family, Julia & Dejuan Perry, Mozella Cottrell, Annastein & Harlteen Stamps, Annice Conaway, Moses Douglas, Edith & Fred Schumacher, Joyce Young, Betty & Sean Madison, Patricia Daughtrey, Vanessa Davis, Audrey& Cedric Bradford, Theresa Richburg, Michael Hinton, Joan & George Mitchell & family, Carol & Dennis Mc Gee, Kameena Reid, Frank Casteneda,Velda Ireland, Patina Allen, Charlie Mae Rattray, Dr. Jackie Johnson, Josie Rockhold, Debra Neely, Gerri Ransom, Anoreene & Thomas Townsend, Erlene & Paul Kennedy, Evangeline Seward & family, Mike Miller, O.W. Wilson, Danielle O' Neil, Dawna Mathieu, Velda Ireland, Karen Held, Tre"Grand Apostle"Hicks, Shelia Baker, David Hanaans, Phil"knowledge"Anderson, Dee Anderson, Carlos G., Debra Shrader, Dr. Patricia Vincent, Dr. Joanna Nachef, Ramona Gifford, David Champion, David Bradfield, Ellie Swanson, Brin Colvin, Craig Kelford, Georgia Cooper, Joan Perkins, Nino Saccomanno, Betty Garcia, Cathy Person, Rev. Tracey Leggins, Opal Johnson, De Etta West, Chuck Franklin, Raquel Benavidez, Jaime Espinosa, Pam Nwachie & Willie Davis (Skin Essence Clinic), Mireya Saldana (Fulfillment Fund), Jubari & Latanya Stewart & Harmonies, Willie Phillips, Jonathon Greer & the Voices of Judah family.

Special Thanks to: Dr. Rosie Milligan—Thank you for being the strong, powerful woman that you are. You have so much wisdom and knowledge to share with the world. Your belief in me and this project means more to me than you could ever possibly know.

Milligan books—I thank everyone on staff at Milligan Books and "Express Yourself" Book Store, especially Queen Sierra, Cedric Milligan, John Milligan Jr., and John Milligan Sr., thank you for your individual parts in helping to make my dreams a reality.

Rev. Candace Cole, I cannot say "Thank You" enough for your great patience, vision, and constant encouragement. I have learned so much. I treasure your ministry, mentoring and friendship.

Jean Ford & family—To an awesome artist, visionary and dreamer. Thanks cuz-let's keep it going strong-Love ya!

Readius and Laurice Hinton, Thank you for being "God-sent" angels, and for plowing my "field of dreams." You are the "wind" beneath my wings.

Michelle & Haree Cornelius—Thank you for your endurance with me through this journey. You have provided a sense of "rock-solid" foundation where there has been very shallow water and Chelle, my sister for life.

Maxine Thompson, Thank you for sharing your expertise and diligence in guiding this project. Working with you has been such a "gift."

Joseph Trower, To "trow" means to think or to suppose. Thank you for encouraging me to keep going, and for your constant surge of fresh ideas. You have such a dynamic gift with people. May every dream you anticipate come to pass.

Rev. L.C. Williams—Thank you for being a dear friend. You have been a great source of spiritual strength and encouragement. May God richly bless you in every endeavor.

Michael Paul Smith, Thank you, my dear friend. It takes much courage and strength to see potential in another human being, and cultivate it to the next level. Thank you ever so much, my mentor, teacher, and friend.

David Dahlsten—To another dreamer, such as myself. Thank you, for allowing me to be a part of your vision-(Rainbow Dancing), and for always encouraging me to never give up on my own. Charles Anderson—Thank you for believing in a dream, and having the courage to help take a part in bringing it to pass. Dumas Martin Jr.,—(Ideas Club-Inland Empire) To an inventor, philosopher, and true artist in his own right. Thanks for all of your encouragement, hard work and perseverance on my behalf.

Marquis Armstrong—To a brother with a strong vision and willing heart. I thank you for your marvelous efforts in helping to put the word out there. May your dreams and visions multiply and send you much increase. Thank you for your excellent commentary, personal input and for putting the word out there: Wallace James Allen, Leta Pazant KRLA radio & Westside Story News, Willie Smith (Bratton & Smith), Benajmin & Nicole Davis (E-N Entertainment) Darryl James (Tenacious Books), Chrystal Allen (Urban Royalty Entertainment), Ian Fox Photography, Gary Ayers (Tri-J investments), Alista ? (L.A. Focus),"P. Wee" (Steve Harvey Radio Street Team), Reginald & Tracey 1460 a.m. radio, Dackeyia Q. Simmons, Erica & Darryl Israel, Daryl Brown, Dr. Gail Sartor, David Mims (DE-LA Marketing & Promotions), Rev. Lee Jackson, Dorothy Mc Farland, Harry J. Lennix, George Rivera, Annya Bell, Rhonda Cobb, Mel Scott, Don Spears, Stanley Tidwell, Ronald Prince, Roy Jackson Special thanks to the ministries that spoke "life" to my dreams and visions when it was truly a need. May God bless and enrich you continually: Bishop Noel Jones & City of Refuge, Candace Cole Ministries, Grant A.M.E. Rev. Leslie R. White, Another Alternative Ministries Rev. L.C. Williams, Evangelist Ford, Bishop Clarence E. Mc Clendon, Rolling Hills Methodist Church, Marilyn Hickey Ministries And to my precious niece, Brittney Mayfield (my wonderful little helper—Thank you so much!): Remember child,

you can be *anything* you choose to be, no matter what anyone thinks or says about you. Choose to be the best! I Love you-
Auntie

About the Author

Christie Douglas, a vocal performer, graduated from California State University of Dominguez Hills. Christie had been musically inclined as a singer/songwriter since the age of eight—and was a music educator with the Palos Verdes Peninsula School District.

She performed professionally with such artists as the late Ella Fitzgerald, Mary Wilson, Shanice Wilson, Debbie Allen, Linda Hopkins, David Foster, and Paul Anka. Christie was a member of the American Musicians Federation and Mu Phi Epsilon professional musicians' organizations. She gained notoriety as a featured vocalist on David Dahlsten's "Rainbow Dancing" and Jubari Stewart's and Harmonies of Praise "Speak Peace." Both CDs are currently available to the public.

Her intimate journey with the characters of *Ecstacy* began in her teenage years. Christie loved to spend hours reading the works of authors such as: Alice Walker, Zora Neale Hurston, V.C. Andrews, Sydney Sheldon, Danielle Steele, and Toni Morrison.

After attaining her music degree, she decided to revisit and complete her manuscript. *Ecstacy,* in essence, is a journey—from ultimate success to ultimate human failure—from the throes of insatiable passions to heartbreaking, soul-searching despair. Experience the *Ecstacy*.

Please visit her website at: www.bflyent.com.

Chapter
<u>1</u>

Sweet Success

N orma Jeanette Richmond smiled proudly, enjoying the view from her ten story Hollywood office window. The towering brick building overlooked the hustle and bustle of the infamous Sunset Boulevard, directly across from the Skybar. The House of Blues and Sunset Plaza were located directly to her left, in plain view.

Large billboards with the faces of beautiful men and women loomed all over her external surroundings. A breathtaking view of the Hollywood hills could also be seen from her slightly tinted window.

Norma folded her arms and tilted her lean body forward. Traffic stood still on a Thursday afternoon, even for the perfectly tanned, tucked, and cosmetically flawless.

Norma's southern roots seemed a lifetime away. What would mama say if she could see her baby girl now?

Norma squeezed her eyes shut, and pictured her mother's bright smile and smooth chocolate complexion. She could still hear her mother's voice so distinctly. "Study hard, gal. Be the best at whatever you do. It pays. God knowed ah' wisht I had."

Norma leaned back in her mahogany chair, reflecting on growing up dirt poor in Virginia. Beans and rice had been the consecutive fare for most nights of the week. Now, almost twenty years later, she was eating and rubbing noses with high society.

She had worked with and even trained some of the best: Veronica Webb, Iman, Naomi Campbell, Tyra Banks, and the list just kept growing. Her name, Norma Richmond, was on the lips of every top magazine editor, film producer, and casting agent in town. Norma's models were always associated with top quality work. They were often launched to new careers in film, music, commercials, their own clothing and make-up lines, or anything that the entertainment world could possibly offer.

Norma specialized in handling the careers of many of the successful Black models, but turned no one away who possessed real potential. Anyone who needed a topnotch, no nonsense, professional model, knew who to dial. Norma had recently been featured in *Ebony*, as one of the most successful and richest Black women in Hollywood, and of her decade.

Norma held out her perfectly manicured hands, and reflected on her mother's hard-working ones. She remembered those hands railroaded with large veins and wrinkles of a woman twice her age. She had worked so hard. Oh, how she wished mama could be with her now.

Her secretary Casey buzzed, whisking Norma away from her miles of thoughts.

"Miss Richmond, Mr. Brookton is here to see you."

"Oh ... what does he want?" Norma thought to herself, sighing out loud. She managed to keep her voice very neutral when she finally spoke into the loud-speaker, "Okay, send him in, Casey."

The heavy wooden doors opened, and in strode Charles Brookton, his shoes making a print in the plush, lavender carpet beneath him. Charles Brookton was a short, caramel-toned, baldheaded man in his early forties. He had been infatuated with Norma since her early modeling days. Norma had never entertained his romantic notions but he had made an excellent business partner. Norma always addressed him by his last name, an idiom he constantly protested but deeply respected her for.

2

"So, how is my most beautiful, favorite lady in the whole world on this most magnificent day?" He took a seat directly in front of her chair.

Norma carefully noted his newly shined shoes, while he adjusted the collar on his perfectly tailored suit. Norma had to admit to herself that Brookton had great taste—in suits that is.

"Hello, yourself Brookton. So, what brings you here?" Norma clasped her hands together and smiled amiably.

Brookton lustfully eyed Norma, smoothing his large fingers across his bald head and shifting his protruding stomach. He was completely enraptured with Norma's look for the day. Her brown Donna Karen suit, chestnut hair, and beautiful oval face flowed so well together. Those bedroom eyes shone like diamonds in a hot desert sand. The tan shell underneath her suit hugged her breasts just right, and the hint of the skirt was ...

"Brookton, is everything okay? You are usually going on and on incessantly about how things are going in New York ... Is something wrong?"

Brookton was CEO of Norma's New York office, and currently overseeing plans for her new site in Northern California. Norma knew that business meetings had brought him to Los Angeles today, and had aptly expected him.

He shrugged his shoulders a bit and then spoke, "Woman, if you don't stop calling me that! How many times do I have to remind you that my name is Charles?" He was slightly irritated that she constantly chose to ignore his subtle advances. He did not worry, she would eventually come around to see it his way.

Norma smiled coyly, but then got right down to business, "No, really Brookton, I mean ... um ... Charles, what's up?"

"Well doll, you know that I could not come to L.A. without stopping by to see my favorite lady. Besides, there's a couple of things I need to speak to you about," Brookton revealed a manila folder from his briefcase.

Norma raised her eyebrows inquisitively, as he continued. "There is this great new photographer I met in town, and I would like for you to meet him. He is young, reasonable, and extremely good. I think that you ought to take a look at his work." Brookton seemed quite sincere. Norma trusted his judgment on these matters, but would not let on too soon.

Norma fiddled around with a few files, seeming uninterested. She needed a new photographer to add new flavor to Ecstacy, and Charles Brookton knew it.

"Well, if I can find the time, I ..."

"Baby, you don't have to find the time to do anything, I have got some of his work right here," Brookton handed her the folder he had pulled from his briefcase.

Norma opened the envelope with caution, trying not to appear too anxious. She took out the five photographs, spreading them like a deck of cards across her transparent desk. She examined them very closely.

Charles Brookton smiled with pride, observing as Norma's eyes widened with excitement. It was the same look he had in his eyes when he had first seen this young man's work.

The middle photograph really captivated Norma. A copper-toned woman, dressed in denim and white, sat on what appeared to be a stairway, against an all-white background. The woman had short coiffed hair, a square shaped face, beady eyes, a keen nose and queenly lips. The incandescent light that embraced her copper tone skin, made her face appear luminous and angelic. This man had seemed to captivate the very essence of her soul. Norma could envision what the woman might have been thinking at the moment the camera snapped. The poignant look on her face led Norma to imagine that it must have been something deep ... something personal. This was the best work that she had seen in months. She had to meet this man.

"This guy is really talented. Set up the meeting," Norma smiled brightly, interested in adding fresh blood to her company.

"Great! I knew you would love it! I will call him and we will meet at your favorite spot, my treat. Call you later to confirm the details." Brookton reached out his hand to collect the photographs.

Norma hesitated a little, but then gathered them together, put them back in the manila folder, and handed them to Brookton. Brookton noticed her reluctance, and nodded his head a little. He knew her well.

"Oh, and uh ... before you go, Charles, how are things back home?" Norma was a little homesick for everyone on Seventh Avenue.

"Sable is really heating things up back home. I told her it would do her some good to visit this office. The girl still needs a lot of grooming, if you ask me. She has picked up some bad habits," he paused, arching his thick eyebrows up and down to get Norma's attention. "But getting on to more important matters ... hey, Norma, if this guy turns out to be hot stuff like I think, would you consider maybe you and I ... uh ..."

"No, Brookton, and I will see you tonight," Norma held in her laughter until he closed the door.

Norma spun around completely in her chair, letting out an exasperating sigh. She gave in to the peaceful solitude of the moment. The afternoon's business was done. Norma negotiated her eyes from the clock, to the growing stack of papers on her desk.

"4:30," Norma said aloud. She would leave early to ready herself for tonight. The stack of papers would have to wait for tomorrow's workload.

Norma paused for a moment, assaying the lavish surroundings of her office. The cream-colored walls, plush lavender carpet, and high ceiling, often made her feel like a queen on her throne. There was a glass door from her office to the inner workings of Ecstacy Enterprises. This included a photography studio, darkroom, three executive offices, a lunchroom and dressing room. All of this, and there still seemed to be something or ... *someone* missing. "Ah, what would mama say, if she could see all of this?"

5

Norma allowed her mind to travel back to the southern Virginia of her childhood. The diminutive abode, which she had once called home, had been a white one-bedroom fixture, resting on one and a half acres of land. The shrubs and greenery surrounding the home occupied most of the living space.

Norma could see her mama, young, beautiful, and smiling bright as ever. Norma would run straight into her arms from school, her apron filled with smells and smudged with the day's fixings. Mama had been a short woman with a voluptuous shape, while Norma's father had been tall, very handsome, and lean.

Marie Louise Johnson gave birth to Norma at seventeen. She and Norma's father, Joseph Richmond, were married shortly before her birth. Juanita came four years later, followed by her baby sister Flora, a year and a half later. Joseph Richmond died when Norma was fifteen, leaving her mother, herself, and sisters nothing but his good name.

Norma had to work to help bring in the money, and care for her younger sisters when her mother was at work. She and her two sisters bonded, and were inseparable in the early years. With the passing years, it was Flora who had drifted. She and Flora had not spoken since her mother's funeral six years earlier.

Marie Richmond had been a stern disciplinarian, and a strong woman of faith. There were three things her "girls" *had* to do: go to school, go to church on Sundays, and get to bed on time. It was her stern hand that guided Norma on the road to her sweet success.

As the oldest daughter, Marie expected more of Norma than from her other sisters. Whenever Norma would become down-hearted, or want to give up, her mother would say, "What do you think cryin' will ever git yah? Look to dah hills from whence yo' help come. Git up off yo' butt and do what you must. You gone be somethin', gal. Yah hear me? I'll see to that."

Marie *did* see to that. With the help of God, loans, grants, and scholarships, Marie struggled to put her three girls through college. This, she felt was essential to their ultimate success.

6

Marie had barely even made it through high school, and wanted better for her "girls." She worked tirelessly, day and night, cleaning, waitressing, and catering to help with tuition and other costs.

Norma quit college at 19, in the mid-80s, to attend modeling school in New York. Marie could not hide her disappointment in her oldest child. She had wanted her to be the first to graduate from college. Marie was too old to really put up a fight, so, she just told her to be the best "damn model" there ever was.

Norma's two sisters did finish college. Flora, Norma's baby sister, got pregnant and married (yeah in that order) right after college, much to Marie's chagrin.

The extravagant wedding ceremony which Marie had always dreamed of planning, was thwarted for a simple ceremony in a small Virginia chapel. Flora was about four months, and her wedding dress fit tight. She still looked like a fairy princess in her creamy flowing gown—Juanita and Norma watching on tearfully as their youngest sister spoke her vows.

Juanita was the one who had never let mama down. She made mama proud by attending the best southern medical school and becoming one of the best doctors in Charleston, Virginia.

Norma envied her smart and younger sister getting a head start on her. Norma was still hitting the pavements of New York when "Nita," as she affectionately penned Juanita, was graduating from medical school.

It was hard for Norma at first as a young, hopeful model on the cold streets of New York. She had nothing but a dream in her heart, and enough hope to last a lifetime. She rented a small studio apartment in Harlem, and immediately went to work.

Over the next two years, Norma caught every audition, agent, and producer she could. She was told everything from she was too dark, not tall enough, not skinny enough, legs too skinny, hair too black, etc. At 5'9, with beautiful dark brown skin and hair, long legs, light brown almond-shaped eyes, sculptured high cheekbones and a curvaceous yet petite figure, she wooed many a photographer. She eventually received the well-deserved attention.

Norma did not listen to anyone who told her "no." She only heard her own inner voice, which always seemed to echo the words of her mother. Then she would call Marie to hear the real thing. "Baby, remembah', it's always darkest befo' dawn. You can be whatever you got courage to believe yah kin'. Now don' you let dem' folks git my baby girl down. It'll be alright after while," Marie would say with a smile in her voice. She always had the right words.

With time, hard work, perseverance, long hours, and the right agent, Norma finally began her steady rise to success. After two years of barely scraping up enough to pay the rent, she started making good money. It started with basic print work and commercial ads, and then finally, a cover for *Ebony*. Boy, was she on cloud nine that day! That was the job that put her in high demand. She was soon featured in *Essence, Vogue, Vanity Fair, Woman's World* and a number of top magazines across the country.

Norma soon became recognized not only for her unique look, but for her promptness, amiable personality and ability to work under any condition. Five years into the business, and she had gained respect and momentum quickly. She was soon working with top models of her day like Beverly Johnson and Christie Brinkley.

Norma was smart. She saved and invested her money wisely. She only rarely splurged, and sent Marie money whenever she could. She only wished she had made more time for Marie. Every time Marie had pleaded with her to come up, she had been too busy, too busy to share her last year. Norma would never forgive herself for not taking out the time.

Norma had no idea how sick Marie had become. Flora was the only one that had known. Then, just before Christmas that year ... her sole inspiration was gone. Norma remembered when the call came. She was on a shoot in Florida when her sister phoned.

"Mama's gone," Nita had sobbed, and a usually composed and poised model, screamed uncontrollably, fainting in the middle of the set. What a black day!

Norma still blamed her youngest sister, Flora, for giving neither she nor her sister Juanita, enough warning of her mother's illness.

Norma cringed now, her insides on fire, as she remembered the awful confrontation on the night of their mother's wake. The entire family of cousins, aunts, uncles and in-laws watched in horror and shock. Juanita had turned her back, talking to guests. Norma had cornered Flora by the kitchen door. Beads of sweat had gathered at Flora's brow, her sister publicly demeaning her.

"Flora, what in the hell were you thinking? Nobody knew the cancer spread but you. She needed us all ... Nita could have ... I ... I could have ..."

Flora retorted, "She swore me to never tell. She said she was gettin' betta ... she swor' it! I bel–believed her ...." Flora had tried to explain, scowling, tears forming in the corners of her red eyes.

Her words fell deaf on Norma's ears. Then, in the midst all of her rage, Norma had said the unthinkable in front of her entire family. "Mama is dead because of you ... you stupid idiot. So, you just try n' see if you can live with that!" Norma had paused for a brief moment, no regrets, coldly walking away. Flora had been left speechless, completely shattered inside. Her light brown face was flushed hot, her eyes flowing with tears.

Juanita had scolded Norma for making such a horrible statement to their sister. Norma had never apologized, nor would she ever forgive Flora.

"My lil' southern flowa," Marie had said of her youngest baby.

Norma's blood boiled when she thought of it now. Norma would never retract her words. She refused to say anything more to Flora. Norma felt that Flora had betrayed them all, watching silently for two months while their mother slipped away. She had to have known that the cancer was no longer in remission.

The day of the funeral, clouds had gathered over the greenery of the Virginian cemetery. Marie had a beautiful burial site, overlooking the whole city, and at the highest section of the mountainous hill.

"Goodbye mama," Norma had sobbed, staring listlessly at the silver casket. To Norma, the white roses, carnations and other beautiful flowers seemed a cruel contrast to the open grave, dirt and debris piled all around her.

She had remained long after everyone else had gone, unable to leave her mother's side, unable to be consoled. She had wept in anguish over her mother's body, imagining the way she must have suffered those last moments.

Norma had taken a short walk, so that she could press her lean body into a huge, oak tree not far from her mother's grave. It sickened Norma to imagine Marie, those last, few pitiful moments, withering away, instead of getting proper hospital care.

Here she had been traveling around the world, making all of this money. All of her newly acquired wealth and fame, what good had it done her! Her poor mama had been dying all along. By the time Juanita found out what was going on and got her in proper care, it was already too late.

Juanita had been more forgiving of Flora, saying that it was what mama wanted, somehow. "Mama wanted to be at home with all her memories," Juanita had said. Norma had been furious with Juanita for saying that, but eventually forgave her. Her perpetual anger towards her youngest sister did not fade, however. Six years had passed now, not a single word between them.

Juanita had remained in touch with Flora, but it was not the same closeness for a long time. Norma had only rehearsed and nourished her anger for Flora over time, only feeding off of its energy. Juanita had made futile efforts to reunite her wayward sisters. She invited them to holiday dinners, family reunions, weddings, and attempted various phone hook-ups. It was all in vain. They managed to faithfully avoid one another, and even politely changed the conversation if Juanita happened to mention the other sister's name.

After Marie's death, Norma gave in to a brief period of seclusion and depression. Friends, colleagues, and respected business associates tried everything to pull Norma out of her slump.

Then, at the age of 28, whether out of desperation, loneliness or fear of becoming a modern-day spinster, Norma married her personal manager, Lawrence Spears. The marriage ended within two years, but not before Norma had endured two miscarriages, public ridicule and humiliation. The press had a field day with their public arguments.

The divorce had not been friendly. Spears walked away with a large chunk of her money, 1.5 million dollars. Norma never even had the time to change her name. In the end, she had lost a good manager, lover, and friend.

Still Norma endured, more determined than ever to not let her dreams fade. When Norma reached 30, jobs were becoming scarce. The younger models provided too much competition. So, with money she had accumulated through investments, and with the help of her broker-turned-business partner, Charles Brookton, she founded Ecstacy Enterprises—an adult modeling school and placement agency.

With her expertise in modeling, business skill, and contacts, she quickly became the most sought after modeling agent in New York. The school turned out many starlets, and business boomed. She opened up a second office on the West Coast in Los Angeles a year and a half later.

Business was going so well, that she decided to allow her partner to control the New York office and relocate to Los Angeles. Two years since the opening of this office, and she was already the "belle" of the ball. Negotiations were underway for an additional office in either Oakland or San Francisco.

Norma ruled her models with the same stern hand with which her mother had ruled. Everyone in New York and now Los Angeles knew that Norma Richmond was the agent with the clout. A model coming with her signature was expected not only to be beautiful and perfectly poised, but timely, friendly, and completely professional at all times.

Norma ironically derived the name *Ecstacy,* through an early life experience. She remembered losing a spelling bee, because she had been unable to spell it. When she went home to ask Marie what it meant, Marie replied, "Why, Ecstasy is like ... like the highest point of feelin' good darlin'. Chile, why you wanna know somethin' like that?"

Norma recalled skipping away in her pigtails, shrugging her shoulders saying, "Ah, no reason Ma'am."

When Norma needed a catchy name for her company, the first word that came to mind was, "Ecstasy." So, she decided to spell it the way she had at that fateful day of the spelling bee in fourth grade, E-C-S-T-A-C-Y.

It all seemed to fit her purpose to perfection. *Ecstacy,* that's exactly how she felt each time she saw one of her well-groomed models on the pages of popular magazines, commercials, videos, and movies. Yes, Ecstacy.

It was funny how little things that her mother had said meant so much to her now. Norma knew that her mother had loved her, and that she was already proud of her accomplishments before she died. She just wished she could see all of this. Just think, a girl from the sticks of Virginia had made good. She had worked so hard for it, and now her mother was not even here to enjoy it with her.

It would do her proud, as Marie would have said. If only she had been given that chance. She could have gotten better. She had just needed Norma to be there for her. Damn Flora for taking that away.

Norma's eyes turned to the large clock on the wall in front of her. Norma called it her "enchantress clock". The actual time read in the tiny lower right corner. Norma could see that it was now 4:45p.m.

The majority of the clock's frame was encompassed by a painting of a beautiful mahogany-toned woman, with shoulder length hair. A tiara, with one single ruby rested over her perfectly oval-shaped head and long neck. She stood posed, scantily clad in blue, a blue background with hints of a dark starry night encompassing her. Norma imagined her to be a queen from some far antiquity, ageless, ethereal. She held out her tiny hands as if to say, "Come to me, my king, let us love ..."

"Till tomorrow, sweet queen. We shall meet again," Norma said aloud, gathering her keys. She took one last look at her office, a sense of longing overtaking her now. Norma finally opened the heavy wooden doors, rushing to meet the afternoon traffic with the rest of the beautiful people.

Chapter
2

Sweet Temptation

"Okay, I've confirmed everything, Larry Parkers in Beverly Hills. And ah ... if you could do 6:30, that would be great. Is that ... ah ... is it good for you?" Charles Brookton cooed unsuccessfully to a preoccupied Norma over the phone. Norma frowned at the clothes she had spread all over her bed. All of the outfits she had tried, nothing had worked for her tonight.

"Uh ... yes, that's good, that's great. See you then ... and ... oh Brookton ..." Norma began, but was now gasping at the dial tone, "What's his name?" Norma paused and stared at the receiver. Oh well, she would have to find out later.

Norma fiddled around with a number of outfits for another half-an-hour. She finally decided that casual, but nice was the way to go for this evening's meeting.

She settled on a mauve colored silk blouse, a flattering black knee-length skirt, and black pumps to accentuate her long legs. She brushed her long chestnut hair into a neat ponytail, and applied a small amount of powder to her face. She then jumped in her gold Lexus to make her journey from her home, off of Silver Lake, to Larry Parker's restaurant.

Norma arrived to find Charles Brookton sitting alone. It was 6:35 p.m. Norma was mortified. Usually, *she* was the one who kept clients waiting. She had fully expected to see the photographer waiting and sweating like a ... well, Norma just loved to make the grand entrance.

"He had better be outside parking his car right now, Brookton," Norma said in an authoritative tone.

Brookton stood like the perfect gentleman that he was, only to gently kiss her soft hand. Norma's heavenly, feminine fragrance enticed him.

"Uh, Uh, Uh, What will it take to make you mine, baby?" Brookton made Norma blush.

Norma recovered quickly, demanding an explanation, "Where is he, Brookton?"

"Calm down, sweet, he should be here any moment," he winked his eye at her. He had a gentle way about him that brought out the soft side of her. It was too bad that he was just not her type.

Norma acquiesced for the moment, and ordered a dry martini. She and Brookton made senseless chatter about the latest industry gossip. They made it a point to keep up on who was doing who, fresh winning faces to watch, cutting edge fashion, top designers of the day, and of course, how the New York office was always at the top of the game.

Charles Brookton always had the numbers to prove it. Norma truly appreciated and respected her friend Brookton, but would never allow herself to admit this to him. Charles Brookton deeply respected and cared for her as well. From the moment he had seen her that night on a London runway, he knew that this woman embodied grace, solidarity, and true beauty in its purest sense.

Norma glanced at her gold watch. It was now 6:45 p.m. Norma could not believe this! She scanned the room, the clamor of glasses and silverware suddenly making her dilapidated nerves worse. She finally called to the waiter to make sure that no special messages had been left. The nerve of this man! Who the hell did he think he was? Norma began gathering her things, as Brookton made useless attempts to calm her.

"Norma babe ... just five more minutes ... give it ..."

15

Norma was determined to leave, "No, Brookton. He surely can't be that ..." she began, but turned her lean body to bump head on into the most gorgeous man she had ever seen in her life.

Jim Sebastian Whaley was 6 feet 2, muscular, with curly Black hair and hazel eyes. His caramel skin and body were firmed and toned from head to toe, with pulsating pectorals, strong quads, and a washboard abdomen. He had a voice that made women squirm, and an endowment that he thought could do the same upon request. He looked Norma over as she rose to receive him. Jim was very pleased with the look of utter amazement on her face. "Yeah, she'll do," he thought to himself.

In actuality, Jim Whaley was a nobody. He was a two bit hustler who only wanted to make a fast buck off of anybody, anywhere, anytime. He grew up on the streets of South Central, Los Angeles. His only loyalties were to himself. His good looks got him this far in life.

He had heard that Norma Richmond was looking for a young, fresh photographer through a friend. This just happened to be the same friend who he "sort of borrowed" photos from, only to pass them off as his own. A few weeks earlier, he had met Charles Brookton at a party. He knew that he was just sucker enough to believe his "hard-knock" life stories. He convinced good ole Charlie to introduce him to Norma. He knew that he could do the rest.

Photography was one of his many hobbies, but he possessed no special talent for it. His main hobbies were making money, and getting women to do whatever, whenever, and however he wanted. He had read articles on Norma and asked around. He knew that she needed a new photographer, and would pay a pretty penny for it. Hell, why not?

" Oh, Miss Richmond, I am so sorry. Traffic was horrible," Jim said scuffling to a chair and wrinkling his brow. He was trying his best to sound sincere.

"It's all right. Just *do not* let it happen again," Norma said, staring into Jim's hazel eyes—his most salient feature.

Brookton smiled with satisfaction. He knew that Norma would like him. Norma struggled for more words, "... Uh, Brookton showed me some of your uh work, Mr. ...."

"Whaley," Jim interrupted, swelling his voice to make it reach that low sexy tone. This always worked well with the ladies. "Jim ... Whaley." He flashed his winning smile. He ascertained from the beam on her face that she was totally into him. Jim and Norma finally took their seats, and the waiter returned. Jim ordered coffee.

"Yes, Mr. Whaley ... um ... I was very impressed by what I saw this afternoon in my office. I could use a fresh new photographer for my agency. Did Brookton fill you in on the history of my agency, Ecstacy Enterprises?" Norma quickly wet her full lips with her tongue, and fumbled her napkin a bit. He looked so delicious.

"Huh, who hasn't heard of your agency?" Jim thought to himself but said, "Yeah, Brookton filled me in a little, but I would like to hear more from you. I mean, it must be hectic running the most successful modeling agency in Los Angeles *and* New York," he smiled deviously. He saw the way that she was fidgeting with her blouse and licking her lips. Yeah, she wanted him bad.

For a moment there was silence. Norma felt as if she and Jim were the only two people on the planet. What was it about this man? I mean, Norma had seen many a fine men in her day, and had even had her share. What made him any different? Why did he affect her in such a way? She kept telling herself that it was because of his talent. She glanced at his strong pectorals, which he openly displayed, and muscular body. She inhaled the mystique scent of his cologne. What a man! Norma touched her chin with the tip of her nail, glazing it down her neck. Jim was loving what her body was saying.

The waiter interrupted, "Mr. Brookton, there is a Henry Cline on the phone for you." Brookton explained that he had to leave, much to his dismay.

He leaned over to whisper in Norma's ear, "Hey don't do anything that I wouldn't."

"Well, that certainly doesn't leave much," Norma roared with laughter. Brookton kissed Norma softly on her cheek, as she threw out her hand in a dismissive gesture. She then turned her body to focus completely on this gorgeous creature in her presence.

Charles Brookton backed away with much hesitation.

Jim noticed the look on Charles Brookton's face, and wondered if there was anything going on between the two of them. "Would I be intrusive to ask what that was about?" Jim inched his body closer to her.

"Oh no, Brookton and I have been friends for a long time. He was only teasing me," Norma explained, but then frowned when she realized what she was doing. After all, she owed him no explanation. She tried to shrug off her intense attraction, and quickly put herself in check. This was a complete stranger. He could be a murderer or rapist for all she knew.

"So, do you think that you would be interested in working for Ecstacy ... I mean, for me? Companies want younger models to sell their products. Young photographers bring out the best in my models. By the way, how old are you, Mr. Whaley?" Norma inquired, her eyebrows raising with curiosity.

"Thirty-two," Jim said confidently, making himself about five years younger. So what, she would never know.

"Oooh, a little bit young for yah, ole' girl," Norma thought to herself but said, "Oh good, we need young fresh blood in our company." She wished she were thirty again.

Jim smiled and nodded, observing her slight blush, even with her dark hue.

"I would like to place you on a trial run for three months. Pay can range anywhere from $150 to $500 for my sessions. depending on the ad and the company we are dealing with. If you are really good, you could make a good living, that is, if you choose to stay at Ecstacy. So, Mr. Whaley ..."

"Oh, please call me Jim," he gently brushed her hand with his.

Norma did not back away from his gentle, warm touch,

"I must tell you ... Jim, if I had known how attractive you were, I would have introduced you to one of my colleagues for some modeling jobs. Ecstacy specializes in feminine advertising, for now. My next branch will probably go co-ed," Norma said, fanning herself a little, "So, Mr. ... uh ... Jim, when would you like to start?"

"Well I don't know. All of this is happening so fast .... When could I start?" Jim said. So much for pride, he needed the money now. This was the best hustle around.

Norma smiled at his quick reply. He was a man who knew what he wanted. She liked that. "There is a shoot on Monday for Vogue. If you can pull this one off, we are in business," she reached out to shake his large, strong hands. Their eyes locked for what seemed an eternity. She then signaled the waiter for the bill. The waiter explained that Brookton had already taken care of it.

"I will see you on Monday, Miss Richmond." Jim smiled confidently. Those teeth seemed to sparkle like diamonds.

"You may call me Norma as well," she said, now rising from her seat. "Oh, by the way ... you do know where we are located?" Norma did not want to leave his side.

"Yes," Jim gazed deeply into her eyes once more, but thought, "Yeah, you stupid bitch, of course I know where it is, who doesn't?"

"Goodbye Jim," Norma sort of sashayed away as if she were floating on clouds.

"Oh yeah, this is going to be easy," Jim thought aloud, stepping outside into the cool autumn breeze.

Chapter
<u>3</u>

Career Plans

Over the next few months, Jim became a dream come true for Norma. He was her best photographer in only a short time. In the meantime, Jim was paying off one of his photographer friends to do his work while *he* assisted. The models always assumed that it was the other way around. Jim always explained that this was a new photographer, and that he was just letting him get the feel of what it was all about. Jim would snap a few shots. Then, his *assistant* stepped in to take those dynamite shots that Norma loved so well. The models were gullible enough to fall for it. Besides, Jim had slept with almost all of them by the end of his three-month probation.

Norma was so taken with Jim that she never caught on as well. The few shots that Jim had taken were always the ones that Norma always threw out.

Jim talked Norma out of coming to his sessions, explaining that it would interfere with his artistic flavor. The models kept their affairs with Jim discreet, fearing that Norma would fire them if she knew that they were boning the boss' favorite guy. Everyone knew how gone Norma was on Jim, but assumed that Norma would eventually find out what a jerk Jim really was.

Jim knew that he could not keep this charade up forever. Norma would eventually discover what had been going on. She was no dummy, just infatuated. That would wear thin soon as well. Besides, paying Winston off was beginning to thin out his pockets. He could be making double the ends he was making now, if only he did not have to pay him money to do the work and keep his mouth shut.

Jim was trapped. He loved his lifestyle. The women, money, fast cars and prestige had spoiled him. He could not lose it all now. There just had to be a way to keep it. What else could he do in Norma's company? Could he tell her the truth? I mean, she liked him well enough to understand, right? Oh, hell no! She would drop him like a hot potato. As powerful as she was, he would never work in this town again. Unless. Unless. A devious thought entered Jim's mind. And that's how change usually began to happen for Jim Whaley.

"Wow, I can't believe I'm really here with you. God ... you finally said yes," Jim teased at Norma. They sat watching the boats and the silvery moonlight shimmer off of the water. Jim knew that Marina Del Rey would provide the perfect setting for a lady like Norma Richmond. Jim had insisted they get an outside seat right next to the water. It was a warm summer night, the gentle breeze enveloping their senses. Jim loved the smell of summer in Los Angeles.

"My goodness, am I *that* difficult," Norma said, half-smiling.

Jim could see that she was a little concerned from the way her mouth cocked to the side. He offered her words of comfort. "No, I just ... I'm just teasing.

I just can't believe I'm finally here with you ..."

"Well, I'm glad you never gave up ...."

"Yes, after the fifth and sixth time I asked ... I guess ... I figured I was doomed ...." Jim recanted. Norma roared with laughter. Jim sighed a little. You know, she really was a class act chick. No woman like her had ever given him the time of day back in high school. Oh, but if they could see him now.

"What I really mean is … this … this is like a dream, Norma. You … are like a dream," Jim attempted to sound as sincere as possible. That should really do it. Damn, he was good. He had to give himself credit.

Jim smoothed his large masculine hand over his silky black hair. He had added a little gel to give it that extra shine. Norma held her hand over her heart and sighed. Her eyes watered a bit. Jim hoped she would not cry.

"Jim … I," Norma began, but was interrupted by the two waiters arriving with their dinner carrying two large trays. "Filet Mignon and Lobster for the lady, and Sirloin for the gentleman," one waiter announced.

Jim hoped Norma was enjoying tonight's extravagance. It was sure costing him a whole hell of a lot. Jim locked his eyes with hers, as the waiter set the steaming hot plates directly in front of them. Norma gazed back just as intently. So much can be said in a moment's glance. Jim knew how badly she wanted him, and was working overtime to be everything she wanted for the time, her fantasy lover, whatever it would take.

They began consuming their meal, and then Norma asked the question that Jim had been avoiding all evening.

"So Jim, tell me *more* about you," Norma added an extra twinkle in her voice.

Jim almost choked on his steak.

"Jim … Jim! … are you all right?" Norma summoned the waiter as Jim gathered his smooth composure.

"No, no … it's okay …." Jim took a sip of water slowly.

"Damn!" Jim thought to himself. How the hell could he tell her more about him? How could he tell her that he had been physically and verbally abused by his own father from the age of eight. Then, when Dad finally left, all of his mother's boyfriends took a real crack at him, "literally." How could he put in "professional" terms, that he had been a ring leader in a Crips gang that had hustled everything from weed to cocaine from junior high all the way to the end of his days at Dorsey High School?

"Jim, are you okay?" Norma noticed his obvious distress.

"Yes ... yes," he lied. He smiled and winked at her, hoping that would put her mind on more *important* matters. It did not.

"So, tell me about Jim Whaley. Who is he? Where does he come from?" Norma braced the filet mignon with her cutlery.

Jim had come up with some rap by then, "Norma, there's not much to tell. I grew up off of Adams and Jefferson. I attended Dorsey High School. I played a little football ... I smoked a little weed," that was putting it mild.

Norma gracefully raised her glass and took a sip of her red wine. Jim really admired the way she did things. She handled herself as a lady at all times. Maybe she would not care about the pictures. Maybe he should just admit everything now.

"A ladies man?" Norma prodded a little more.

"Uh ... I wouldn't say that," Jim lied again. He and one of his buddies had once made a bet to *personally handle* the entire cheerleading squad. Boy, were those the days.

His looks had always been his best asset. He had lived with a few broads after high school, giving them the loving they needed for the roof over his head. He had only held one job consistently in two years—a bartending gig. He had also ventured into a few gigolo gigs, but no chicks as classy and high profile as Norma. He got tired of that really quickly, and the women would not stop calling. No, he needed a steady thing, and Norma fit the bill just fine. He knew that to convince Norma Richmond, he had to give the performance of his life.

Three months later ...

"Oh! Oh! Oh JI——M!" Norma cried out as her body convulsed all over in a final climax. She smoothed her hand over Jim's sweaty back and kissed him passionately. "Jim, I've never felt like this about any man in my life. I think I'm falling in love with you," she cooed, holding him tightly and glancing up at her legs entangled about his hips. She laughed a little at her vulnerable condition. She no longer cared, she was in love.

Jim smiled slyly and caressed her gently. "Norma, I think I love you, too. I've been thinkin', you know. There is no other woman that I would rather be with than you," he lied with ease, pausing to give her that sincere puppy dog look.

By this time, Norma had turned her back to him, and was now eyeing the clock. Jim would not let the heat of their last moment together pass, "Norma Jeanette Richmond, will you marry me?" Jim kissed her back ever so sweetly.

Norma turned to look at him, tears welling up in her eyes. He almost felt guilty. She looked so happy, and he knew that she loved him. It was a shame. He had tried to love her. She was certainly a good woman.

"Yes! Yes!" Norma clutched his neck so tightly that he choked a little. They both laughed and then embraced. Norma could not believe it! She thought that this could never happen to her. It had all happened so fast. They had only known one another for six months. Ever since that first day, she knew that he was the one for her. What can you say when it's true love? She knew that there was something special about Jim since that first moment. He was talented, gorgeous, and he made love to her better than any man ever had. Sure, she knew that he had flings with a *few* of her models, but things would be different now.

Everyone had tried to warn her about him—Brookton, her sister, the models, even her lawyer. Norma was determined, and she was now in love. He was going to be all hers. She would make him a better man.

At first, it was just pure attraction and business. Jim took photos and got paid for his excellent work. The sparks were always there, but nobody ever made the first move. Then, one day Jim asked her out to dinner. She refused of course, but Jim was very persistent.

Norma finally acquiesced to a very romantic dinner at Marina Del Rey Pier. The moonlight reflected off of the ocean's view, as they gazed into each other's eyes. Jim looked exquisite in his creamy top and tight dress slacks. From that night on, Norma agreed to continue seeing Jim, as long as they remained discreet. So, they had dated every weekend from then on. And now, three months later ... Dah dunt dah da—all dressed in ... oh surely not in white. Mama would turn over in her grave if she wore white.

Norma began meticulously planning the details of her wedding in her head. Jim interrupted her thoughts with a sultry, luscious kiss.

"Come back, my love. Where have you been?" Jim whispered softly.

"I was just ..."

"Save the fantasies for the two of us okay, baby. In the meantime, I just got a page that my client, *our* client, is there. So, save it for later," Jim slipped from underneath the covers.

Norma pulled the covers over her head, allowing herself to reminisce on the first time they kissed, and the first time they made love. What a lover! He had been so gentle, so sensual. Norma got flushed all over, as she recalled how Jim had coaxed her over to his apartment that night.

Norma had jostled the door to Jim's apartment, only to discover a darkened room, lit only by five tall red candles. There had been a setting for two, sparkling champagne, a dozen red roses, a bowl of fresh, juicy strawberries, and a lobster dinner.

"Jim," she had called out, a little breathless. She yearned with anticipation.

"Jim," she had called out again, a little nervous this time.

Jim had magnificently appeared, pushing open the bathroom door. There he was, a blue bath towel barely clinging about his waist. His perfectly toned body, flat abdomen, nipples and silky hair were dripping wet. He summoned her to come inside, saying nothing, but enticing her with his provocative stare and pouching lips. Norma's mouth stood ajar. She had never seen a man more gorgeous and seductive in all her years. He looked positively edible, standing there, wet, dripping, calling to her in the dark. Norma was convinced that she was in some erotic fantasy or dream state from which she never wanted to wake.

Norma took one step closer. Jim smiled. It seemed as though he were ready to engorge her with those soft pinkish lips, and hazel eyes. Jim motioned seductively with his fingers. Norma had not wanted to give in to lust too presumptuously. She wanted to control the moment, but Jim had made that all but impossible.

Norma's knees surrendered to a weak sensation, as she dared edge closer to her waiting lover. Jim managed to grab one of the wet, juicy strawberries from the nearby table. Norma kissed Jim softly on his wet lips, and closed her eyes, inhaling his clean, masculine scent.

"Ummm," Norma moaned, noticing the growing rise from beneath the robe.

"Jim, I ..." Norma began her 'let's wait' ... speech.

"Shhhh," Jim placed a finger over her pursing lips. He then bit provocatively into the strawberry, chewing slowly. Norma felt as if he were biting into her very essence.

"But Jim, I ..." Jim entwined his tongue with Norma's. She too could taste the delectable sweetness of it all. Before Norma could voice any more protests, she found herself lost in the smoothness and serenity of his dripping arms and chest. Norma helped him to dry, while he led her backwards towards the bedroom.

When the time for actual lovemaking came, Jim ravaged Norma's body with succulent kisses all the way to the bed.

Jim was a few years younger, but a master in the bedroom. He was so in tune with what her body wanted and needed. He lit her body with electric passion and fire, touching and satisfying every dark and deep part of her, reaching into the crevices of her very soul.

"Now girl, you are truly rich," she giggled to herself aloud. All of the money and success in the world could not make her feel the way Jim did. God, how she loved him.

*   *   *

Jim smiled as he walked away, content that his plan was working so well. He had only intended to get close enough to secure a position, and maybe eventually tell her the truth. This would be the best position of all. He could not understand how a woman so smart and business-savvy, could be so stupid when it came to men like him. Didn't her mother ever tell her, or something? I mean, it wasn't as if he had anything against her. He genuinely liked and respected her. He just was not in love with her. Who married for love nowadays, anyway? No, this was a pure investment.

Chapter
<u>4</u>

Lights, Camera, Action!

"It was great to see all of the celebrities out for this event. The ceremony was just ... just absolutely incredible. Norma looks beautiful this afternoon," an entertainment reporter smiled brightly into the camera.

Norma had allowed the media a small platform outside where the wedding reception would be held. They could remain, as long as they promised to stay out of the way, and near the platform. Norma had been explicit about *her rules*, no one dare cross her.

The ceremony had taken place by the lake, the scene so peaceful and calm as she hoped her marriage would be. Friends, family, and a host of celebrities gathered to show their support. Juanita had been the maid of honor, while a few of her best models had served as bride maids. Reporters from *Entertainment Tonight, Extra* and all of the news channels were there to report the spectacular event. Norma decided not to make it hard for herself by trying to hide it from the media. When rumors began to spread around, she called the media herself and offered her *conditions*. She decided that it would be great publicity for her models, who paraded their Armani wedding attire like Amazon princesses.

Norma's gown glittered as if it were made of constellations, with its cream colored shade. It had a long flowing train which seemed to extend into forever. The bodice was embroidered with silver etchings, and lace sleeves rippled out as if it too were a part of the watery scene where the couple had made their vows earlier. Her tall, Victorian style collar reached up to meet the top of her long neck. Norma's traditional veil crowned her cascades of curls wrapped around a tight ball in the center of her head. Her make-up had been administered by her favorite make-up artist from Ecstacy, Brenda Donovan. Brenda had done wonders. She had been so excited, and did not get much rest the previous night. The bags which had collected under her eyes had now disappeared.

"I can not believe my big sis finally tied the knot. I thought you would end up an old spinster," Juanita teasingly said, her tall legs and short haircut making a strange combination to Norma.

"Oh you little peanut head. Are you and *this* one serious?" Norma said, pointing to her new beau standing aloof and looking rather lost amongst the crowd of celebrities.

"Well, I duno," Juanita shrugged her shoulders and sauntered away. Always the kidder. She had hoped that she would finally meet her match. God knows it would take a helluva man to deal with her, she knew, she had helped to raise her.

Norma sighed as her mind's eye pictured Marie, and how proud she would be of them both today. Deep in her heart she had wished that Flora could be there too. She feared the gap had bridged too deep to repair at this point, so she simply ignored her sister's suggestion to fly her down for the wedding.

Juanita had been quite surprised when Norma did not explode in anger at the mention of Flora's name. She knew that it was only hurt that kept she and her baby sister apart. Juanita knew that Norma would eventually have to resolve those feelings.

Norma took in the breeze of the exhilarating spring air. This had always been her favorite of all seasons. Everything seemed to be alive, and perfumed with the fragrance of life itself. This place had such a character of its own. Norma was suddenly unaware of everything and everyone around her, allowing herself to indulge in this perfect moment.

Her eyes focused towards the tranquil marshy lake which was about half a mile away from where the ceremony had been. The lake was enclosed by huge rocks of white, gray, pastels, pale greens and creamy smooth colors. Milky white swans floated in the distance, their heads held high and proud. She felt as proud and beautiful as those swans this day.

Norma's mind shifted back to the ceremony. The beautiful daisies the girls had used to decorate the chairs and veranda seemed to shine with adulation and anticipation. The sun made its perfect shimmer off the waters of the lake, and it seemed to reflect the light which had entrenched her soul. She felt like the luckiest woman in the world.

Norma felt the magnificent presence of God in this beautiful garden of light. Norma saw Him in His work. She felt a twinge of guilt for not having a traditional church wedding, as Marie would have wanted. She observed this beautiful scene, smiling inwardly. She could see Marie smiling in approval, saying, "You dun good, gal. Shol' nuff dun good." A tear trickled down her cheek.

"Hey, why is my beautiful bride crying?" She looked up to see her handsome husband smiling. Jim looked like a bright angel in his white tuxedo. He had been given a male facial and shave about a week before the wedding. A little fuzz was once again starting to appear. He was such a man's man, so masculine, yet sensitive and sexy.

"I am crying because I am the happiest woman in the entire world."

Jim held her hand and kissed it with his luscious, brown, wet lips. Truly, this was the happiest day of her life. Jim decided to let her revel in this moment, embracing her gently from behind and kissing her softly on the cheek.

"Later, love," Jim whispered softly. Norma caressed his cheek with the back of her hand.

"I love you so much," Norma whispered back. Jim did not respond, closing his eyes and sighing instead. Why did she have to be so into this thing? So into him? He did not deserve that. Jim turned his body away from Norma to greet guests, just as she wanted to embrace him again. Norma felt a cold chill up the nape of her neck, but shook it off gently.

Jim soon turned the guests over to Norma, and snuck away from the crowd to take a smoke. Norma hated these things, but he needed one now. He looked at the whistling trees in the restless wind. The evening air was turning the breeze a bit colder now, casting shadows where the light had dwelled all afternoon. He stood there trying to convince himself that he had done the right thing.

Jim suddenly became distracted as a woman's voluptuous figure caught his attention. He did not recognize her. She must be one of the new girls. Wow! She was hot! After his honeymoon, he had to be *sure* to get back to work.

He almost felt guilty as he noted the look of euphoria on his new bride's face—almost. He threw his cigarette to the ground, and smashed it with the bottom of his foot. His thoughts were interrupted by a rough grasp on the shoulder. He turned to face an angry Charles Brookton.

"I know that *you* didn't take those damn pictures, Whaley. Your friend fessed up. Guess you decided to stop paying him. It's over Whaley. Once Norma finds out, she will drop you like a hot potato," Brookton followed Jim, as he walked apathetically away. Realizing that Brookton would not buzz off, Jim suddenly turned towards him. Guests were beginning to notice. Norma would notice soon, if he did not respond.

Jim faced his opponent with an ice cold look of pure evil. It sent chills down Brookton's spine, who swallowed down hard.

"Who do you think she will believe, Brookton?" Jim said, calmly waving at passing guests. "Do you think she will believe you over her husband?" Jim turned his palm towards his wife.

Brookton looked at Norma, so blissful, so content. He did not want to see her hurting. He knew that she would find this joker out. She just needed time to escape his spell. Brookton hoped it would be sooner than later for all of their sakes.

"It's just a matter of time before she finds you out Jim. That's a helluva woman you have got there, and I would not want to be the one to cross her," Brookton's voice cracked from the pain in his heart. He hurt for Norma. He hurt for Ecstacy. He hurt for himself. This fool did not deserve her love. Brookton pushed Jim out of his way, thrusting his way out of the garden. He would apologize to Norma for leaving later.

Jim sighed, happy that his tough guy bluff had worked. He knew he could count on good ole Charlie to keep it a secret a little while longer. It would give him enough time to find some security in this thing.

After all, Norma had smiled and blinked her pretty little eyelashes, as he grit his teeth and signed that prenuptial agreement. He would find a way around it. He always did.

Jim once again became distracted by another beautiful model in front of him. She turned to face him. Her soft brown complexion, long hair and heavenly eyes were a needed distraction at this tense moment. They laughed and talked as Jim rubbed his hand up and down her side.

Norma searched through the blaze of reporters for her husband. She had tried to say hello to Brookton, but he had looked a bit distracted. She wondered what was bugging him.

Norma finally spotted her husband, embracing Cherrie, and her smile immediately turned to a grimace. Norma sighed, and folded her lips tightly together. He would change. She knew he would. He just needed to adjust to being married. She stopped to stare at her wedding band. "He is all mine now," she thought to herself and then began frantically waving to Jim.

Jim remained oblivious until she was close enough to touch him.

"Jim," Norma called gently as he pulled away from the model to be at her side.

"Norma, baby ..." Jim tried to explain.

"Jim, I have been looking for you all over. It's time for pictures. You, of all people should know how important that is.

32

They have to be perfect, because this day is perfect," Norma embraced Jim and gave Cherrie a dirty look. The model was so embarrassed that she had to excuse herself.

The wedding party gathered around as the reporters and television cameras made their own photo album. Norma could not see or hear the flashing lights or watching cameras. Everything seemed to continue in slow motion. She focused her eyes and heart on Jim, this man that she would spend the rest of her days with.

She thought of the new house she had recently purchased, and how surprised Jim would be when he saw how beautiful it was. She wanted to fill that house with their children and grandchildren. She could hear the echoes of small voices in her mind. To think, she would have given Marie grandchildren as well.

Norma's mind drifted to the passing years that would lie ahead. She pictured Jim's beautiful curly hair, with patches of silvery gray. Oh, she was sure he would be just as handsome as he was now. She wanted so much to make him as happy as he had made her.

The world stopped for just one wonderful moment, as they posed for the first time as man and bride. The flashing lights seemed far away to Norma. She could not see the worried look on the face of her doting sister. Juanita had been carefully surveying Jim's actions since she had stepped off the plane.

Norma could not hear the applause of the crowd, nor the sound of the tipping wine glasses and voices of congratulations. All of Ecstacy and the industry watched as she embraced her new husband. There seemed to be no one else in the world besides Mr. and Mrs. Jim Sebastian Whaley.

Norma and Jim spent seven days on the sandy beaches of Waikiki, Oahu. For the first three days, they played in the sand and made love by day. They danced under the spring moon by night, enjoying their first Luau as a couple, romantic moonlight dinners, and skinny-dipping. At first, it seemed too good to be true. Jim was every romantic fantasy come true for Norma. This did not last for very long. By the fourth day, Jim's flirtations began again. Norma also noticed that he was drinking heavily. He had even started smoking. Was she doing something to make him unhappy? Was it her fault that he was beginning to act like a jerk? Who was this man? He was not the man that she had married at all. All of the qualities that had attracted her—his wittiness, intelligence, sensitivity, and lovingness, disappeared down the barrel of that bottle. She would suggest that he seek counseling for it, when they returned home.

Norma soon became really homesick. She called in to both offices every morning and night, and then made a few calls to her sister, Juanita. Brookton had said that everything was running smooth in New York, but sounded tense. She wondered why he was acting so strange. Her correspondent in Los Angeles, Debra Winey, said that things were fine, and that everyone missed her terribly.

Jim constantly complained about her insisting to check on business while on their honeymoon. It hurt Norma. He should understand how much she loved her work. In fact, he had complained about a lot of things lately. He had seemingly changed overnight. Norma kept convincing herself that if she gave it enough time, things would work themselves out.

The final day of the honeymoon arrived, and Norma was glad to see it. She awoke early, determined to enjoy this last day despite him. She turned to find her husband already gone. "Good," she said aloud.

Norma slipped from underneath the warm sheets and wandered over to the balcony. She pulled back the screen, and walked out to view the splendor of the beautiful beach scene before her. The sun was already on the horizon, revealing a breathtaking and picturesque view.

There were only a few surfers meandering in the bluish-green waters off the Hawaiian coasts that morning. Norma perused the baby-blue cloudless sky. Her eyes scanned all the way down until the sky blended with the endless streams of blue ocean. She sighed as she marveled at the beauty of the sea. The sea, with all of its mysteries and ironies, was life-giving, yet life-threatening. Its movement was continuous, yet ever-changing and unpredictable. A huge wave engulfed one surprised surfer. He laughed vicariously, quickly swimming in to shore with the rest of his friends.

Norma could already feel the warmth of the sun's rays in the morning light. She inhaled deeply, as if she were inhaling the entire ocean in one breath. She decided that the best way to begin her day would be a morning run on the tan sandy shores. Norma made her way to her hotel bathroom, still yawning and wiping the sleep from her eyes.

After Norma had showered and dressed quickly, she glided on to the lobby and smiled at the clerk, grateful that no one had recognized her. After all, the success of Ecstacy had brought more attention to her as a public figure. People seemed to want to know more about her now than when she had been a model. Funny, all she had wanted in those early days was to be recognized, noticed. Now, she edged away from public attention, and everyone wanted a piece of her. The press, which had paid little attention to her in the early days, now loved her. She had been featured in various magazines: *Essence, Ebony, and Vogue.* They all loved to tell her rags-to-riches story.

Norma opened the side screen door of the hotel, which opened to a sunny, warm day on the beach in Waikiki. Her feet seemed to sizzle from touching the hot sand, so she decided to wear those tennis shoes she had brought just in case.

A few couples were holding hands and walking along the mouth of the beach. She wished that it were she and Jim, walking along as if there were no one else in the world. It was easy to see how much in love they were, even from this distance.

Norma stretched her long arms and legs in front of her, preparing for her morning run by the surf and sun. Norma stopped short as she heard a woman's roaring laughter coming from nearby. She scanned the beach for the source. Then, she heard a familiar voice edging the woman on. She walked a little further on the sand, curiosity having taken a strong hold of her. It seemed to take forever to find the source. Where was it coming from?

Finally, she stopped in her tracks, clearly identifying the strange familiar voice. There, to her chagrin, was her beloved husband laughing, embracing and fondling a yellow, wavy-haired, bikini clad woman on the sandy beach. Jim turned the woman towards him as if to kiss her, when he met with Norma's angry stare. Jim's brown face actually turned a shade of red. The woman turned around, her smile quickly turning to a look of sheer embarrassment.

A pain shot up Norma's spine, and she suddenly became breathless. She looked down at the sand, as if she were lost somewhere in a far away desert. It was their honeymoon, and he was already ...

Norma began to run through what now seemed an endless ocean of sand, back in the direction of the hotel. Jim left his new companion to hurry to his wife's side, searching his mind for some reasonable explanation. He had come too far to ruin things now.

Norma made it into the hotel, and into the elevator before Jim could reach her. She ran straight to the room, and into the bathroom, slamming the door shut. Norma shook her head and cried, trying not to believe or remember what she had seen. Norma shuddered to think of what she might have seen just a few moments later.

Her mind scurried into a sea of endless thoughts. How could he, right there on the beach. His behavior had been heading in this direction. She should have known it. She knew now that she had made a horrible mistake. But why marry her? Did he want money? After all, he had signed the prenuptial agreement that her lawyer had drawn up without any reservations.

Norma's thoughts were interrupted, as she heard the door to the hotel room open. Jim was breathless from running after her, "Norma, baby please come out. We can talk about this like two adults," Jim leaned against the bathroom door.

"Talk about what! You can't change what I saw!" Norma yelled, sounding much like a spoiled child. A quick memory from her childhood flashed. Her mother would spank her, and she would run to the bathroom repeating in a monotone frenzy, "I hate you, I hate you," until she fell asleep. She felt like doing that now, but Jim kept talking.

"Baby, I love you," Jim said pleadingly.

"Go tell that to your whore!" Norma checked to be sure the bathroom door was locked and sank down on the closed toilet seat. Her tears made her face hot and eyes began to swell. She buried her head in her hands to weep.

Jim continued talking and begging for her absolution for what had to be an hour. He finally tired of talking. Soon, there was an odd silence. Norma stopped crying, exhausted from all of the emotions spent. She closed her eyes and fell asleep.

Norma was awakened several hours later by what sounded like a soft whimper coming from the outside. Norma rubbed her eyes, still raw and swollen from the tears.

"Oh, he's gotta be kidding," Norma chuckled a little. She splashed some water on her face, before slowly unlocking and opening the bathroom door. She peaked out.

The lights were off in the room, and she caught a glimpse of the sun seeping in through the closed screen. It was late afternoon by now, the sun almost ready to set. Their last day gone to waste.

Norma opened the door completely now, only to examine Jim, curled up in a fetal position, by the wall. His tears flowed like a newborn baby. He looked up at Norma with tear-filled eyes. A surge of pity flowed through Norma, too strong for her to ignore.

"Baby, I am sooo sorry. I don't want to lose you. I love you so much. I swear, I will never even look at another woman. Just please forgive me," Jim pleaded, making his masculine voice sound innocent, almost child-like.

Norma searched for the right words, her mouth dry and bitter from all of the crying and screaming. She was speechless. No man had ever begged her for anything, much less cried for her. He must love her after all.

Norma knew much more about how to deal with a man on a business level. She had had to be tough as a man to succeed. Her brief marital experience had given her no real preparation for this. Here was this beautiful man begging her in the dark for her forgiveness and love.

The afternoon sun blazed in from the screen, casting a glimmer of light to cast on Jim's hazel eyes and hair. Jim looked much like an angel in the afternoon's light.

Norma crept over to kneel down beside him, smoothing her hand over his silky hair. She then bent down to sensually kiss him on the forehead. Jim looked up at Norma, as she gently wiped the tears from his eyes. Norma slowly knelt down beside him, kissing his lips slowly and softly, again and again, until the kisses became longer and wetter.

Jim's maleness responded, as Norma pulled him on top of her long supple body. Their tongues collided, becoming joined in harmonious rhythms of love. He entered her immediately, diverging deep inside of her, riding her smooth and gentle. He made her body shiver all over with pleasure. With each stroke he gave her more and more pleasure, making her cry out for more.

Jim had always been a great lover, and this time was no exception. They rested a while, then made love again and again, well into that night.

Jim looked over at a sleepy, satisfied Norma, the moonlight now seeping through the shade of their suite. He let out a sigh of relief.

Jim wondered what his little wavy-haired yellow friend was doing now. He reached in his pocket beside the bed to find the number he had managed to scribble down earlier.

Norma moaned and searched for her husband's body with

one hand. He noticed the sweet, serene look on her face. Jim smiled, pleased with himself for what he had done. He could now be grateful that he had taken those acting classes in high school.

Chapter
<u>5</u>

Business As Usual

"Close your eyes," Norma teased at Jim, as they pulled into the driveway of their new six-bedroom home. Jim reluctantly obliged her. "Okay, now you can open them," Norma parked securely, removing the key from the ignition.

"Oh, Norma, you act as if I have never seen a hou ..." Jim cut his sentence short, beholding the most magnificent house he had ever seen.

It was a castle compared to where he had been living, an apartment right off of Sunset, close to the office. Their new home stretched over 4,290 square feet, with its perfectly manicured lawn, ample garage space, and three marble steps leading to the front door. It was a dwelling fit for royalty.

Norma was pleased at the look of utter amazement on her new husband's face.

Jim could even see hints of a spacious backyard, with its magnificent view of the Hollywood hillside. The infamous Hollywood sign could even be seen in the distance.

Norma quickly got out of the car, as Jim followed at her heels.

"Norma baby, wait up for your man," Jim grabbed at her from behind.

"My man is walking a little too slowly. You gotta keep up!" she teased.

Jim smiled, but inwardly complained. He hated it when she did that. Why couldn't she just let him be the *man* once in a while? Why did she always have to have the last word?

Norma opened the door, and Jim began to tussle with her, "Like it or not woman, I am carrying you over the threshold."

Norma's vivacious laughter filled the block.

"Jim, weren't you supposed to do that at the honeymoon?" Norma struggled to adjust her long body in his arms, as they tread the marble steps leading to their doorway. They managed their way into their new home just in time for the phone to ring. Norma rushed away from Jim's arms, answering the phone by the fourth ring.

"Hello," Norma spoke into the receiver, a little breathless.

Jim walked around in a daze, checking out the place. One thing about this chick, she sure was classy. Jim admired the work that she had already put into the place. It looked as if she had begun to furnish and everything. Jim settled himself in front of the thirty six inch wide-screened television set, not far from the fireplace.

Norma grinned, watching her husband wander from room to room like a child at Disneyland. Norma refocused on the business at hand, "Hello ... what? Well, can't it wait for a couple of days? I just got back from my ... oh, I see ... yes ... well, okay," Norma shook her head in frustration.

Jim sighed, noting the look on Norma's face.

"Oh no baby, don't tell me, not business, not tonight. I wanted to check out our bedroom," Jim playfully cuddled her in his arms.

"I am sorry sweetheart, it was Charles Brookton. He says it's urgent. He says he needs to talk, and that it can't wait. The office isn't very far. I should be back in no less than two hours?"

Jim shrugged his shoulders a bit, "Well, I know how important your business is to you. Just try to hurry back, " Jim kissed her softly on the lips.

Norma was still swarming with heat from their passionate night of love making on the last night of their honeymoon.

"I will try to hurry back," Norma kissed him back and gave him one last look of love before heading to her meeting.

Jim let out a loud sigh, "Ah, whoosh! You done it now, boy!" He pretended he was dunking a basketball into a hoop. "You done it now, boy! You hit the big time!" Jim watched, as Norma pulled her Lexus out of the driveway, leaving him alone to enjoy their new home.

Jim ran up the stairs, as if he were a child at Christmas, running to catch Santa Claus. Jim froze on the second story to the upstairs, when he suddenly realized what his wife had said. She was going to meet Brookton! Oh no, he had come too far to let that fat jerk ruin things now. Jim quickly ran down the stairs to call a cab. Norma had said they would go to his old apartment, and trade in his old car soon.

Norma walked into her dimly lit office to find Brookton sitting behind her desk. Brookton stood when she entered the room. He looked rather grim.

"Oh, Norma hon, I'm sorry, I was just ..."

"Never mind that Brookton. What is this about? I assume you would not just leave your post in New York to discuss the weather. What is it?" Norma took off her coat, and enfolded her arms.

"Norma, I was going to let this wait until you settled in, but I just could not stand it another minute," Brookton began.

"Sounds serious," Norma took a seat in front of her own desk, as Brookton remained standing. She had never heard him sound so anxious, so unsettled. Was one of her models in trouble? Was it Sable?

"Norma, it's about Jim ...." Brookton thought he should be the one to tell her. When the cookie started to crumble, he did not want to get thrown out in the trash with the garbage. "Norma, Jim never took any of those pictures. He lied to us both," Brookton charged.

"What? What are you saying?" Norma shook her head in disbelief.

"Jim hired a guy by the name of Winston Thompson to take them for ..."

Jim kicked open the door, and marched in, "Norma, don't you believe a word this son-of-a-bitch says! He told me he's in love with you, and that he'd say anything to get you away from me!" Jim rested his hands on the desk to catch his breath. He had run up the flights of stairs to her office.

Norma looked from Jim to Brookton, "Brook ... I mean, Charles is this true?" she looked at him intently.

"I ... I ... Norma," Brookton sputtered at Norma, peering deeply into her eyes. He could not deny that he had feelings for her.

"Norma ... you ... you have known me for all of these years. Are you really going to believe this fool over me?" Brookton struggled, as Jim smirked. Norma twitched her eyes from Brookton to Jim, and back again. She did not know what to think.

"You trust me, don't you? You believe what I am saying?" Brookton retorted.

Jim shook his head at him as if to say, "I told you so." Jim's words at the wedding echoed clearly now in his mind like a sounding church bell.

"Who do you think she will believe?" Jim had said. Looking at Norma now, he knew that he had been right.

"Brookton I ... I really don't know what to think ... I ..." Norma began. She knew that he would never deliberately lie to her. Maybe he just had a few facts wrong.

"You will have my resignation on your desk in the morning." Brookton walked away in embarrassment and hurt.

"No, please! I need you! Ecstacy could never run in New York without you! Don't do this!" Norma pleaded as she had never before.

It was true. Norma could not have left the care of her company to anyone else. He had been so loyal and faithful. He had nothing to gain by deliberately deceiving her. Yet to choose to believe him at this moment over her own husband would destroy her marriage. She could not give up on it that easily.

Charles Brookton paused for a moment, contemplating her words. He turned to face Norma, her beautiful face all contorted with worry and uncertainty. She would have to uncover the truth on her own. He was confident that she was strong enough to endure.

"Looks like you have all you need right there, baby," Brookton nodded his head towards a delighted Jim. "Good luck," Brookton poignantly raised his eyebrows. He then opened the heavy wooden doors and slammed it hard behind him.

"Brookton, no! ... you can't do this!" Norma stared at the door, as Jim tried to console her.

"Look, baby, we don't even need him ... I can even run it for you if you need ... " Jim said. This could be just the chance he had been looking for, a way to the big cheese.

"Jim, honey, I ... I don't know, that's a lot of respon ... " Norma began.

"Damn Norma! You treat me like I'm not a man! Give me a chance to prove myself. Who the hell else can you trust at this point?" Jim pressed a bit, seeing that his words were registering. She was definitely considering his point.

"Well, maybe for a while, just until I can talk some sense into Charles Brookton," Norma said tentatively.

"Baby, you won't be disappointed," Jim smiled and planted a wet kiss on Norma's hand.

"Well ... I had better not be ... I can brief you on some things ... just for a couple of weeks ..." she hesitated. She was still trying to convince herself that she would be making the right decision. Jim was right, what other choice did she really have? Jim smiled, pleased that she was seeing things his way now.

"See you later, sweetheart," Jim smacked her lips, and pranced towards the door.

Norma called out after him, "Jim, one more thing before you go."

Jim could hear the lingering question in her voice, "What babe, what is it?"

Norma hated the way he called her babe, "Jim, I have to know ... was *any* part ... I mean any part at all ... of what Brookton said true? You did take those pictures, didn't you? He was wrong somehow ... wasn't he?" Norma raised her eyebrows, anxiously awaiting Jim's reaction.

Jim's face seemed to turn another shade of brown, "Norma, I can't believe you would take his word ...."

"Jim ... I have to hear it from you," Norma still waited for his answer. She was not going to let him off that easy.

"Look, I told you the truth, Norma, what else do you want? Brookton lied. You know, I may not be the classiest guy you ever met. But you are gonna have to learn how to treat your man with a little respect," Jim walked away, slamming the door behind him before she could even respond.

"Jim!" Norma called out in vain. "Damn!" Norma sighed, hitting her hand hard on her desk. Norma closed her eyes and took a deep breath in. She wanted to believe Jim more than anything in the world. She had never known Charles Brookton to lie to her. Maybe he just had a few facts twisted around.

Norma leaned towards the window to view the night sky. The electric lights of Hollywood glamour shone across the strip. She peered curiously from her window, as a black stretch limousine pulled in front of the hotel down the street. Norma could see a lithe woman with her glittery gown being assisted out of the vehicle. She knew that it must have been some celebrity, from the flashing cameras and gathering reporters. She could not see the face from where she was standing.

It was strange how normal life had to go on behind the scenes, as the glamorous and glitzy life maintained itself. It was part of Hollywood's strange allure. The illusion must remain intact. All hell broke loose for somebody somewhere, while the "star" shone and smiled bright for all admiring eyes. In this town, everybody wanted to be "somebody."

Norma sighed at her own newest dilemma, "Mama, I sure need you now. Oh, how I need you." Norma watched, as Jim stepped inside the cab that had been waiting outside for him. She sighed and took a deep breath, inhaling the cool, brisk air.

Months passed rapidly by. Norma kept telling herself that things would eventually get better with Jim. Just as he had done on their honeymoon, Jim was wonderful at first. He was all too caring, loving, and compassionate. Then, from one day to the next, he changed into this philandering drunk.

Norma's sister Juanita warned, "He's only there for the money and position girl. I'd sure watch my back if I were you."

Norma appreciated Juanita's candid nature, but it sure hurt like hell to have her say it that way.

Hopefully, Brookton would make his return sooner than later. Norma had tried everything to convince Brookton to return. In the end, he decided to take a leave of absence rather than resign. However, he did not say when he would return. Ecstacy needed a body to fill the position. Brookton had left Norma no other choice. Jim would have to do.

She would do the major footwork from her Los Angeles office, and commute whenever necessary. Jim would merely serve as a representative of the office that he held, attending meetings, and making minor executive decisions.

She would brief Jim and advise all of her people in both offices to report every idle move that her husband made. Their marriage was one thing, but her business would not crumble at the hands of Jim Whaley.

A few weeks before his departure to the New York office, Jim was more distant than ever. Every time she turned her back, he was flirting with one of the models. The pictures he took were not his usual high quality work, and he drank so much that it made Norma worry.

His public behavior toward her became a constant source of humiliation for Norma. It got to the point that they could no longer appear in public together. Rumors of his affairs were running rampant at Ecstacy, the tabloids, and aboard. She was losing the respect of clients and colleagues. People were talking all around town. Norma was losing her edge.

The last straw was an embarrassing instance at the company Christmas party at the Beverly Hilton.

Jim wandered in, more inebriated than usual that evening. He was haggardly dressed in a dirty, thin polo shirt and slacks about two sizes too tight.

Norma sighed noticeably, watching her husband make his grand entrance. He spoke extremely loud, almost tripping over the beautiful Christmas tree, so meticulously decorated with greens, reds, silver and candy canes. Lou Rawls bellowed his rendition of the Christmas song. Norma and her staff exchanged gifts and shared pleasantries and tales of Christmas past.

Everyone paused, peering on in horror, as Jim clapped out of sync, almost losing his balance. "Wooooh," he screamed out ever so inappropriately. Norma froze, pouching her lips, and enfolding her arms.

Jim was becoming increasingly more disgusting. Her mind briefly ventured back to what had first attracted her to him—his confidence, style, and smoldering good looks. This man who graced her presence now was a complete stranger. There was no sign of the Jim Whaley she had fallen in love with.

"Hello, dear, thought you'd miss me ... so ah decided to join you." Jim grabbed Norma's hand, smacking it with a rude kiss. Norma snatched her hand away.

"Jim ..." Norma began to admonish him.

Jim began to serenade his wife, his singing voice screechy and unpleasant, "So ... ooooh ... ther ... e she is ... Miss Amer-ica ... she's exch-aanging gifts an' toys ... she's Mi ..." Guests glared on, speechless and embarrassed for Norma.

The security guard intervened to talk some sense into Jim, "Man, won't you go sit down somewhere. Here, let me help you to a seat." Jim resisted, as the guard attempted to grab his arm.

"Look, brotha', I got this! I can handle it!" Jim almost stumbled again, but managed to regain his balance.

Norma excused herself to the restroom, her face flushed with shame.

"Norma, babe! Where yah' goin', girl? It's time to pa—rty ... uh ... uh," Jim motioned and wiggled his behind to the imaginary beat in his head.

The entire staff remained silent and frozen. It was as if Jim was the only one alive in a room filled with sculptured stony statues. Jim absorbed all of the attention. He felt a rush of excitement in his veins. Finally, he was the center of attraction. He had come to resent being in her background. He hated being—Mr. Norma Richmond Whaley.

A few stood with their mouths and eyes open wide. Everyone wondered how a graceful and beautiful woman like Norma Richmond, ended up with such an idiot.

Norma ran the water from the sink, splashing a little on her face. She then stared at her reflection hard in mirror. Norma allowed her eyes to circle with the bulbs of light surrounding the mirror, lights much like those on a dressing room mirror. Hollywood encompassed her, it was always everywhere.

Her eyes had begun to water a bit, but she fought back the tears. She would not let him get the best of her, not tonight, not ever. She had worked too hard for that.

Norma gathered her composure when Teresa Cummings, one of her long-time executive staff members, entered the restroom. Norma braced herself for the coming speech.

Teresa was terse and frank, "Girl, what are you gonna do? That is a fool you got out there."

Norma thought for a moment. How should she respond? No matter what their working relationship had been in the past, she was still the boss.

"I've got it under control," Norma shook her head a bit and adjusted the collar to her red leather jacket.

"Oh, I can see that ..."

"I said, it's okay, Teresa. I'll deal with Jim when I get home. Now ... we have guests waiting," Norma paused, taking one last look in the mirror.

Norma was intent on remaining calm and completely composed, no matter what Jim did. She was the daughter of Marie and Joseph Richmond. She could do anything.

Norma stood there for a moment, seeming to draw some inner strength from somewhere deep inside. She finally exited, feeling lighter and ready for Jim's chicanery.

Norma approached the scene, pausing for a moment. She grit her teeth in disgust at Jim—unbuttoning his top, and slinging it across the floor, much to the delight of greedy onlookers. Norma's face remained unscathed and cool. She gracefully apologized to guests, and collected her husband. They exited the front door with Jim eyeing her curiously. Norma signaled to the valet to bring the car.

"Baby, why you do that? I mean, I was enjoying myself ..." Jim began snapping and wiggling again.

Norma perked her top lip, as if she had tasted something unsavory and sour. She shook her head at him, as the white Escalade was parked directly in front of them.

Norma made her way to the driver's side, and quickly braced herself behind the wheel. She opened the door, as a stumbling Jim was practically carried and helped into the vehicle by two attendants.

Norma stared into the steering wheel of the Escalade. She had bought this car for Jim. If he kept going this way, he would kill himself while driving it. Jim rested his head on the seat, as Norma pressed her foot hard on the gas.

"Jim, I seriously think you should consider getting help for your drinking. This isn't the first time ... you embarrassed me in front of my entire staff ...."

Jim raised his head, glaring at her with a look of disgust, "Woman, don't you take that tone with me. I don't care who they were. I am your man ... and while you suggesting I get help, why don't you get some help from work-a-holics anonymous or somethin' ... since that's all you like to do!"

"Somebody has to pay the bills," Norma rolled her eyes at him, giving him a condescending look. Jim rose his hand to slap her, but stopped abruptly, his hand frozen mid-air.

Norma slammed hard on the brakes, jerking the car to the side of the road. She glared at Jim directly in the eyes, "If you ever rise your hand against me, I promise you will be in jail so fast ..."

"I know, I know ... look ... I'm sorry ... So ... I had a little too much to drink. Baby, I got lonely, so I came to find you ... Come on, baby ... what's happening to us? We had fun once ... didn't we?" Jim implored, rubbing his fingers against her warm skin.

Norma had to admit that he was right. All they did was argue lately. Jim was leaving for New York the next week. Maybe the separation would do them both some good.

"Come on, baby. I'm leaving next week. Let's try to make the most of it."

Norma pulled off on the Mulholland exit and headed towards their home. She just wished they could get through one peaceful day without arguing, or him drinking, or complaining about her work.

Norma's mind revisited the faces of her staff and colleagues. She had never been more embarrassed in her life. Norma glanced over at her husband, barely able to keep his eyes open, drifting into sleep.

They had once been so happy. Norma thought that nothing could separate them. She briefly recalled the tranquil scene at her wedding. Everything had been so beautiful—the swans, the lake, the flowers. Where did it all go wrong? If nothing else, Jim's departure would help her to redefine some peace in her own life.

Norma parked the white Escalade in front of their home. She nudged Jim to wake, but he had begun a low snore. He would not budge. Norma quickly made her way from the driver's side to

Jim, and placed one of his strong arms on her shoulders. She balanced him with her own lean body, guiding his steps as they walked.

"Le, oh Lisa baby ... not like that," Jim muttered in and out of consciousness, his head now bobbing back and forth. Norma's heart sank, but she kept moving up the driveway. She wanted to leave him, muttering and all, right there in the driveway. How he disgusted her.

Norma knew there had been other women, but she certainly did not want to hear all the gritty details. She struggled, anchoring his body with hers, up the long driveway. They finally made it to the three marble steps. Norma lifted Jim, shifting and grunting to get them both up those steps.

They finally made it to the door. Norma stood in the dark, fumbling for the key. Sleeping beauty awakened right on cue.

"Um, a ... where am ... Oh Norma, what's going on babe?" Jim mumbled and made strange sounds with his tongue.

Norma refused to reply, but rather shook her head at him. He barely maintained his own balance, grabbing the top of his head and grimacing as if he were in pain.

Norma finally managed to get the key in the door, and shove it open. She left her muttering husband outside in the cold, dark, while welcoming herself to their warm abode.

With Jim leaving for New York in one week, there was much work to be done. Norma and her staff had briefed him on expectations. There was paperwork to sign, and this occupied most days, along with meetings. Jim felt fully prepared for the job by the time his flight landed at John F. Kennedy Airport.

With Jim gone, Norma dove more into her work, making her office her haven. She came and went, only using her home to bathe and sleep most of the time.

Back east, Jim found more women and more booze to conquer. His new position only gave him more ammunition against Norma. He hired a new lawyer and crooked accountant to change the books, so that Norma could not keep up with his strange spending habits. He continued to place blame for the ills of their marriage entirely with Norma.

Jim began to despise Norma now. He blamed her for every unhappiness of his miserable life. He only made necessary appearances in Los Angeles, making a separate existence for himself in New York, independent of Norma Richmond Whaley.

Norma was at least spared from Jim's humiliating behavior in his absence. She began to once again gain the respect of her colleagues and staff. At least Jim could not completely ruin that. Then, just when she thought she had a handle over her situation.

Six months later ...

Norma sighed relief as she finished her last bit of paper work for the day. Finally, it was time to go home. She glanced up at the clock, 6:35 p.m. She wandered to her favorite spot at the window, gazing up at the warm evening sky.

It was the end of another hot summer day on Sunset Boulevard. It would be an early day for *her*. The secretary's buzz interrupted her thoughts.

"Mrs. Whaley, there is a Miss Brandon here to see you."

Norma frowned, unable to recognize the name, "Uh, I'm sorry Casey, I didn't know that I had any further appointments today. Can you tell her to reschedule? It has really been a long day."

"Miss Richmond, she says she does not have an appointment, but I believe you should see this young woman. I don't think it would be a waste of your time," Casey said, a strange hint of excitement in her voice.

"All right, but this had better be good. Send her in," Norma inwardly complained. She hoped this would not take long. Norma stretched and rubbed her shoulder with the palm of her hand. She then made a mental note that she needed to make an appointment for a massage.

The door opened and in walked a woman Norma thought destined to be the next Veronica Webb. Dollar signs popped into Norma's head, and she was no longer tired.

"Hi, my name is Kimberley Brandon. I am new in town, and heard that this was the best place to come to start a new modeling career," Kim said, her sweet, innocent country-like tone.

Kimberley Evette Brandon stood 6 feet, with wavy brown hair, hints of sandy-colored streaks, light brown skin, and green eyes. She had a perfect shape, that could make men bow to their knees. She had the sweetest voice and the most beautiful, innocent face.

Kim Brandon was already perfect in Norma's book— perfectly marketable. Norma tried not to look too excited, while dollar signs danced around in her head. She could already see her on somebody's cover. Ideas overflowed Norma's excited mind.

"Well, we will have to work on the accent, but the rest works," Norma thought to herself, motioning for her to have a seat.

Kim sat in delight, carefully examining every move that Norma made.

"You came to the right place. I am sure we can find some work for you," Norma seriously underplayed her hand. She knew that Kim was a potential goldmine, but she could not appear anxious. She was certainly glad that she had come to her first.

"So, tell me about your work experience. Have you found an agent, yet?" Norma pried a little more.

"No, I am really just starting out. Here is my portfolio, though. Tell me ... Miss Richmond ... Do you really think I have a chance?" Kim said smiling brightly at Norma. She handed her a brown folder.

"Poor naive thing, she really has no clue," Norma thought to herself but said, "Maybe so, dear ... but tell me... how old are you?"

"Twenty-four," Kim maintained that perfect smile, her eyes gleaming.

Pose after pose and cover after cover flashed through Norma's mind, as she flipped through Kim's portfolio.

"Well this is good ...very good. You have a definite appeal, but a slight hint of innocence about your look ..." Norma began as Kim pretended to focus intently on everything that she was saying.

Innocence and Kimberley Brandon should never be mentioned in the same sentence. She had never known her father, and had lived with her mother in a small town about 50 miles outside of North Carolina. Her mother died when she was twelve, leaving her with no known relatives. An orphan, she had been passed from one foster home to the next, staying in trouble at school, smoking, drinking, even trying out a gang for a while. She was raped by one of her foster parents at fifteen, so she decided to run away.

Kim vividly recalled the stormy night she had gathered a handful of clothes, and stuffed them in a small duffel bag. Thunder sounding like a thousand horses crashed against the roof of the small home. She could hear large footsteps advancing towards her door slowly, slowly ....

"Kim," Norma noticed the far off look in her eye.

"Yes," Kim's body jerked a little. Norma scratched her forehead, a little intrigued with this little one in her presence.

"If only she knew that she now had the world at her feet. Every magazine in town wants to photograph a woman like her, her perfect skin, bone structure, eyes, and hair," Norma thought to herself with a twinge of jealousy. After all, it had been so hard for her to gain the acceptance which Kim would so readily receive.

Kim smiled with satisfaction as she watched Norma's expression. She knew exactly what Norma thought about her, and that was exactly what she wanted her to think. Oh poor, naive, helpless little Kim!

Kim knew exactly what she was doing. Kim wanted the money and career that Norma was willing to offer her. But she wanted more, much more.

"Listen it's late, but I would really like to get you started as soon as possible. Can you come in say ... Friday for me to show you around?"

"Yes," Kim said very bright eyed and anxious, twisting her head a little so that her cascades of curls fell a little in front of her shoulders.

"Another cover girl pose, Ching! Ching!" Norma thought, but said, "Nine o' clock sharp." Norma firmly shook hands with Kim. It all was set. Kim smiled, her mind racing one hundred miles a minute.

"Get ready for the ride of your life, Norma Richmond," Kim thought to herself as she and Norma walked out of the office.

Kimberley Brandon raced home to her small, cramped studio apartment in the center of downtown Los Angeles. She knew that Norma had been impressed. She had practiced what to say, what to wear, and how to walk for months. Her whole life had seemed to prepare her for this very moment.

She had arrived in Los Angeles just six months ago. Norma had been on her agenda from the very start. She opened the door to her cramped, unfurnished studio humming, knowing that tonight had been her lucky night. She hurried to her bathroom to take out the green contacts and false eyelashes which were beginning to make her eyes itch.

Kim sighed as she pondered all of the pictures of famous models she had on her walls—Iman, Veronica, Beverly, Cynthia, and now there would be Kim!

Kim focused in on the large photo she had enlarged of Norma. The picture was about the size of a painting. It featured a much younger, smaller, picturesque Norma, in a fashionable bathing suit and black sun glasses. A white scarf covered her head, as she wandered the sandy shores of some far-away tropical wonderland.

Kim visualized herself in that same setting, how she would look, stand, what she would wear. Oh, it would be magnificent!

Kim now picked up her own portfolio, kissing it and smiling brightly. "We are gonna make millions my darlin'. All our dreams are finally coming true," she said aloud, her conjured accent fading.

Chapter
<u>6</u>

Friends

9 a.m. sharp. Punctuality was important to Norma. Kim had to be on time. 9:01 a.m., Kim stumbled a bit, stopped a minute as if to put on a new character of poise, grace. She opened the lavender doors to find Norma and her photographer, Jeffery Wilcox waiting. Norma smiled graciously and said, "On time, I like that."

Norma unlocked the door which led to the inner walls of Ecstacy Enterprises from her office.

Jeffery teased, "You are getting the royal treatment. It's not often she gives the tour herself."

Norma let out an exuberant laugh, "Oh Jeffery, stop it."

There was no fabrication in that statement. There was something about Kim. Norma knew that she would make it. Norma had seen many girls, and was responsible for many of the big success stories within the last five years. She had yet to see her on these professional cameras, but she had a feeling that she would not be disappointed. Kim had more than just a pretty face. She had that raw desire, an ambition that could not be hidden from a woman like Norma. They looked nothing alike, but she recognized that hunger, that ambition. She had to give her a chance.

"I'd like to try you for this ad for *Essence.* The editor is waiting for the proofs," Norma said matter of factly.

Kim knew that she was talking about the editor-and-chief of *Essence* magazine. "This is just gonna be a little test. Oh, forgive me for being so rude. This is Jeffery Wilcox, Kim," Norma held out her hand in a queenly gesture. Jeffery miraculously appeared. Kim wanted that kind of power.

"Jeffery, this is Kimberley Brandon," Norma waited patiently, they both nodded and smiled in greeting.

"Now, Jeffery, I want you to treat her right. This could be one of our newest super models. Kim, clothes are in the back. I'm going to leave you two for a couple of hours. I have some things to do in my office," Norma glanced at her watch, waving a hand at Jeffery and Kim, then leaving.

"The clothes are hanging on a rack in the back. Feel free to dress while I load the equipment," Jeffery said, gathering his equipment and adjusting light for the shoot.

Jeffery looked around to see Kim standing at the door of the dressing room holding up her clothes to barely cover her naked body, "Oh, dear ... this is not a nude scene. There *are* clothes to put on in the back," Jeff laughed a little to himself while loading his camera.

"Models," Jeff shook his head. Jeff heard a loud noise which startled him. He turned around again. This time, he saw Kim, now *completely* naked, standing near the scene where he had previously shot another scene. She used her finger to signal him to come over.

Jeff stood there in awe and wonder. He marveled at her perfectly shaped and sculptured body, perfect in every dimension imaginable. My, what a gorgeous woman she was! She smiled as if she knew exactly what he was thinking.

The lights from the scene gave her creamy brown body an even more translucent and radiant glow, making her appear something more than human. Jeff could hardly contain his

58

passion rising, as he moved towards this magnificent creature before him.

"Are you sure that's what you want me to do? Get dressed?" Kim said pursing her lips. Jeff placed his equipment on a nearby table, while a small conflict arose in his mind. What if Norma walked through that door, right now? His career would be ruined.

Jeff glanced back up at Kim who was now provocatively licking her crimson lips and motioning with her finger for him to join her.

Jeff could no longer resist, "Oh, what the hell!" he thought aloud, advancing towards her now much as a panther to a kill.

Kim now held her hands behind her back. Jeff gently touched and kissed her shoulders, her skin was soft and smooth as silk. Kim revealed what she had been hiding, a bright red condom. She handed it to Jeffery. She placed her diminutive hands inside his massive, strong grasp.

"Models," Jeff said once again, allowing himself to become locked in Kim's embrace.

She searched his strong back with the tips of her fingers, all the way down until she reached the bottom of his shirt. She helped him take it off, as he led her to the bed on the set. She tantalized him with soft, succulent kisses that led all the way to far away places and then back again.

Kim was an attentive lover exploring every section of his masculinity until he moaned with earnest desire. He responded to the pleasure she gave him, when their tongues met with hungry passion. Kim sensually kissed and whispered in Jeff's ear as he searched and prodded her. He finally entered her with throbbing erotic pleasure, delighting her succulent body with every stroke. Kim felt up and down his firm body down to his buttocks, while he occasionally stole simple kisses and softly caressed her breasts.

"Oh KI——M!" Jeff yelled out as he climaxed a half-hour later. His body collapsed in exhaustion, but he still managed in a soft kiss or two. "Oh babe, that was incredible," he said a little embarrassed. This had not happened on the set like this before. He would be fired on the spot if Norma found out about this. He looked at Kim, her hair a little tossed about, her caramel skin glowing with sweat. She looked exquisite. He hoped this would not be just a one time thing.

No sooner had they finished their session of lovemaking, the sound of a woman's heels was heard in the near distance. They both scrambled to clothe themselves. Jeff thought of how his career would be ruined, as Kim calmly reached for a skirt she had left on a nearby chair. He wondered why she did not seem as concerned. Whatever the reason, she sure was sexy as hell!

A tall thin pecan colored woman emerged from the hallway. She was clad in black leather, with a long reddish mane, her strong definitive features apparent even in the darkened room. "Oh, it's only Sable!" Jeff thought aloud.

Sable Jennings was twenty-five years old, and had been the number one girl at Ecstacy up to this point. She had flown in from New York just two weeks ago. She had had a few trysts with Jeffery herself back in the day, but never on a set like this. He was losing his composure. She laughed a little at his obvious embarrassment.

"Damn girl, you scared the hell out of me!" Jeff yelled.

Sable could no longer resist the urge to laugh, "You should 'ave seen yah face, man, look like yah seen ah' ghos'," she smiled letting out a hint of her West Indian roots. Sable knew that if it had indeed been Norma walking through that door, they would have both been fired on the spot. Norma was cool and everything, but she did not play when it came to work.

"Let's get to work Kim, before she ..." Jeff noticed that Kim had already disappeared into the dressing room.

"You mean, finally get tah. look like you already been a' workin' man, eh," Sable said, quite amused. She roared with enthusiastic laughter.

Kim emerged five minutes later, poised and absolutely

beautiful. She was ready to work. Sable backed away, but studied Kim carefully. Kim was an absolute natural with the camera. Jeffery could not help wondering with each shot, if she would see him again afterwards. He was already hot for her again.

"Oh! the prints were absolutely superb!" Norma exclaimed, practically gasping with excitement and enthusiasm.

She and Kim stood grinning auspiciously in Norma's office, as the editor regaled over what she was viewing via speaker phone. Taylor finally released the line, while Kim smiled to herself. Norma explained further details about what the next move would be.

It was no surprise to Kimberley how pleased Norma had been with the shots. With Jeff there to pick the best shots, and brag on her level of *professionalism*, how could it ever go wrong?

Norma quickly took Kim under her wing. She became her best protégé after that first shoot. Kim had "cut her teeth" as Norma would say, and had proven herself as a viable commodity.

Norma began teaching Kim everything that she needed to know in order to have a long lasting career as a model. Norma poured valuable knowledge into Kim, everything from beauty tips to how to properly market and package your look.

"It's a cut-throat, ever-changing industry. You have to know how to survive it. Play the game, and play it to win," Norma would tell an all too eager to listen Kim.

Norma also taught Kim personal ideals of ethics, honesty, and integrity. These were qualities that made Norma a magnet in a business such as this one. People knew that when Norma gave her word about something, it was as good as done. She taught Kim to project the same aura.

Norma further advised Kim on how to dress, what to say, and to conduct herself in a way that would guarantee the client's continued service. Kim became her best student and someone she eventually called "friend." She soaked in as much information as she could. They went everywhere together: shopping, lunch, and even some board meetings. Norma wanted Kim to be business minded, not just a working model, washed out at 30. Norma enjoyed having a prodigy. It gave her a new lease on life, since Jim had been away in New York.

Jeffery Wilcox pursued Kimberley with fervent desire after their short tryst. Kim dated him a few times, but made it very apparent that she had no intention of an affair or long term relationship. She had got what she wanted, and was finished with him. He had served his purpose. Because of his excellent work and excitement about her, he had more than sold her to Norma. Norma had sold her to everyone else. That was all that was necessary. He was dispensable.

Kim was soon on every cover of most of the popular magazines around the country, and soon internationally. She was quickly becoming the "it girl" at Ecstacy, and even had offers for film.

Kim always arrived at her sessions timely, rested, prepared and friendly. She was the rising star at Ecstacy, and Sable soon began to feel the descent of her own falling star. Unknown to Norma, Sable and Kim had been hanging out every weekend partying.

Kim had noticed the nasty coke addiction that Sable could not seem to get a handle on. At first chance, Kim mentioned this to Norma, and had even warned Norma about Sable's reaction when she found out. She was only being a concerned *friend*.

One day, it all hit the fan as Kim sat in an intense power meeting with Norma in her office. Sable stormed through a mortified Norma's office.

"What the ..." Norma began.

"Mrs. Whaley, I couldn't stop her," Casey marched in after.

"It's okay Casey, I can handle this," Norma smiled reassuringly at Casey.

"Yah scandalous bitch, Yah had to leak dah story, didn't yah!" Sable yelled at Kim as she sat coolly with a slight smirk on her face.

"Who do you think you are, storming into my office?" Norma managed to get out some of her own anger. Could they not handle this on their own time?

Sable pointed her finger dead in Kim's face raging on, "Your trusted friend here leaked dis' story to dah tabloid peoples." Sable held up two papers with identical headlines: "Sable Can't Kick Coke Habit." Sable's brash voice had echoed down the corridors of Ecstacy by now, and Norma could hear people assembling and asking questions right outside the door. She had to put a stop to this quickly.

"Sable, you can't just ..." Norma began as Sable charged at Kim, grabbing a piece of her lengthy curly locks. Kim managed to untangle her grasp, and shove Sable to the carpet. Sable reached for Kim's hand as she fell, and Kim tumbled down with her.

By this time, all of Ecstacy had gathered at the door. They cheered on as the two women clawed at each other like wildcats, rolling around the carpet, pulling and scratching at each other. Norma and a security man finally managed to pull the two women apart and separate them.

"It tain't ova, bitch!" Sable managed, breathless and struggling to get away from the strong grasp of the security guard.

Kim braced herself, preparing to give all watching eyes a meaty performance. Her clothes and hair were tattered, and mascara was running down her face. The tears streamed as she cried out, "I don't even know what you are talking about! I would never take a part in what she said! I was only concerned about her!" Kim begged for sympathy from the crowd. A few onlookers gathered at Kim's side, as Sable heaved with unrepentant anger. They all shook their head at Sable now.

Norma could care less who did what, this circus parade had to be stopped. "All right, everyone out!" Norma shut the large wooden doors where they all had gathered like black crows to a corpse. Only she, Sable and Kim remained. Norma would reprimand her nosy staff later.

"Sable, we have all known about your uh ... problem for some time," Norma began. She grabbed Sable by the arm and took her to a more private section of her office. Kim gathered her composure after her ordeal.

"Look Sable, we have discussed this before ..."

"Yes, Miss but ...."

"I have given you chance after chance to get help. I have even paid for your rehabilitation ...."

"She did it on purpose! Tha traitor! Me know she did!" Tears streamed down Sable's cheek. She stood to lose everything. Ecstacy had been good to her over the years, rescuing her from a life of hard core drugs, stripping and prostitution. She could not go back that route.

Kim had only befriended her to betray her. She could see that so clearly now. She had needed a friend so desperately, and had secretly desired to be intimate with Kim. When Kim mentioned hanging out, she just assumed that she knew what was expected. How could she have been so stupid?

All Kim wanted was her spot in the limelight. She could not understand that there was room enough for both of them to taste success. Sable knew now that Kim was a female tarantula, and would destroy anyone that got in her way. She had to warn Norma, for her own sake.

Norma embraced Sable. She truly felt for the girl, but she had warned her to take care of this problem. How could she think that it would not be found out. Whether Kim leaked it or not was unimportant. Now, it was not only all over the tabloids, but reputable stations were confirming and carrying the story as well. Norma's name and reputation were now on the line.

Norma had first heard the news when she walked in that morning, from a few reliable staff. She always had her people keeping about five steps ahead of everyone else in town. This gave her an unsinkable edge, and all things remained intact.

Kim had come in a few moments later, to make her confession about hanging out with Sable, to express concern about her growing drug problem.

Norma's expression turned perplexed, as she watched Kim now. She had once again opened the wooden doors, becoming engulfed in the sympathies of her waiting fellow models. She remembered how Kim had acted so concerned for Sable earlier.

Norma knew as she looked over Sable's shoulder, and into the faces of her colleagues and models, that the verdict was already in. Her own executive staff would compel her to let Sable go. The girl needed to get her life in order. Maybe when she finally got it together, she could come back.

"She do you dah the same, Miss Norma," Sable mumbled through her tears.

"She is a she-wolf, and she will betray you, mark mah words," she said as Norma shook her head. Norma looked from Sable to Kim to the faces of her entire staff. Yeah, the girl had to go.

Kim smiled proudly at herself as she viewed her reflection in Ecstacy's restroom mirror.

"One down, more to go," Kim adjusted her lipstick and running mascara. She exited the restroom, heading back down the darkened corridor. She would make another star studded appearance, before going home to her new upscale place on Wilshire Boulevard.

"Kim," she stopped and sighed, recognizing the puppy dog voice calling from behind her.

She turned around to face a love struck Jeff, "Oh, Jeffery, how are you? You know I was going to call you ..."

"Oh yeah, that's what you said last week. You know Kim, you could have told me you were not interested. You really are one number Kimberley Brandon, and I will be glad when Norma finds you out. You are nothing but a two-bit tramp and a user," Jeff snarled at her. Kim turned and walked away.

"Takes one to know one!" Kim yelled out with her back turned. Jeffery had already disappeared around the next corridor.

"Poor guy, just can't take a hint," Kim mumbled to herself as she made her way down the hallway.

Chapter
<u>7</u>

Betrayed

"Okay, love turn aroun' a' bit," Timothy Simons said, pushing back his blond hair and adjusting the lens to the camera to meet with Kim's radiant smile.

"Oh, that's great! Do it again," he said, as an inebriated Jim Whaley stumbled in the front door. He stopped to retain his balance, as he struggled with his blurry vision.

"Damn, I have to stop drinking so much," he mumbled. Simons turned to greet him with a look of disgust.

Jim Whaley had just returned to town from New York, his position, as chief executive over Ecstacy Enterprises returned to Charles Brookton. It had all been decided in a phone conversation between Charles Brookton and Norma. The next thing you know, Jim was sent packing. He completely resented her for pulling the rug from under him. Norma's relief that the company was back in "capable hands" was all too apparent. Jim had not been in town a week, and already his partying and drinking binges had begun.

Timothy changed his roll of film, and adjusted the lights. He turned his head only to see Jim stumble his way around the studio. He had known Norma for quite some time now. What had she seen in that smuck, anyway?

Simons quickly resumed his work as his attentive model entered with a change of outfit. Kimberley Brandon. He would remember her name. She reminded him so much of the young.

Norma Richmond: so talented, responsible, bright, and sexy as hell. He had met Norma early in her career on a photo shoot back home in London. He remembered that day as if it were yesterday.

It had been Norma's first day of shooting, on a cold London shoot almost fifteen years ago now. He distinctly recalled how afraid and vulnerable she had seemed. Norma had appeared with her bright red blazer and tight leather pants. She was so gorgeous. After those first few flashes of light, Norma's tension loosened. Those dynamite poses began, and that smile!

Kim whipped her body around for another stunning pose, grabbing his attention once again. Norma had been right about this one. She photographed even better than Sable, without all the hassle and dope.

Jim mumbled something to Timothy and began to unload the materials he had managed to bring. He was supposed to be assisting Simmons with Kim's session today. Norma had Simmons flown in from London for the session, due to Jeff's lack of enthusiasm about working with Kim.

Norma's words had cut Jim like a knife that morning, "I don't know Jim, your photos are just not what they used to be. Why don't you just help Timothy out, today." She had been so patronizing. She was really starting to annoy him again.

He also hated Norma for firing Sable without consulting him. He realized early into the gig, that it was strictly in "name only", and that he possessed no real authority. Sable was the last straw. She and Jim had been lovers in New York. He had only sent her out there to get a taste of L.A. He had warned her to kick the dope habit. Norma must have discovered the affair, and booted her out. It was as if she was trying to take anything and everything away that gave him pleasure. He was tired of her bitching about his drinking. She was not his mother.

There were rumors that Norma had been secretly meeting with her lawyer, Jonathon Newman and Charles Brookton to offer Jim a reasonable divorce settlement. Once Norma found out about Jim's strange book-keeping and spending habits, it was only a matter of time. She wanted out of this marriage.

Word had gotten around to Jim from his little playmates at the agency, once he returned in town. Jim really wanted to do better, but was so far gone, he could not pull himself together. He blamed Norma for neglecting his needs, and making him feel less than a man. All Norma ever concerned herself with was her "business." He too wanted out. But what would he do and where would he go without this marriage? He would once again be a nobody, lost and forgotten. Norma would come out smelling like a rose, as she always did.

Jim began to make his way to the restroom to gather his thoughts, when ... Red alert! Stop the press!

"What a dame!" Jim thought aloud. Kim threw back her long wavy hair and posed for Timothy.

"Okay, baby, now give me that million dollar smile. Yes, baby, that's it, love!" Timothy was delighted that she responded so well. She seemed to know exactly what he wanted.

Jim altered his route to ask the identity of this beautiful swan standing before him. He tried to get Timothy's attention.

Timothy's British accent roared out as he reprimanded Jim for disturbing his work, "Say there, can't you see that I'm trying tah work. Some of us do af' tah work for our living ole' chap." Timothy gave Jim a sly wink, but by then, he had already slammed the restroom door.

Jim splashed water on his face and smoothed his shiny black hair with his hands. He stared at his eyes, all red and watery from his drinking. He held out his hands in frustration, "Nobody at this damn place respects me. I'm not a man, I'm a ... a ... a pawn!" Jim shouted aloud, a sobering sickness descended upon him as he rushed inside a bathroom stall.

"Take a break, dear. You've been workin' hard all afternoon," Timothy smiled, pouring he and Kim a glass of iced tea.

"Was that Jim Whaley?" Kim asked as Timothy nodded.

He only confirmed what she had already known. She recalled seeing his picture in Norma's bottom drawer. He was much more attractive in person.

Norma had not seemed very interested in filling her in on any details about her husband or her marriage. Kim remembered the look of contempt on her face, when she had asked about him. There was not a warm feeling conveyed.

"Yeah, that's him," Norma had said with disgust. Kim had learned early on not to mention Jim's name, since it put her in a foul mood so quickly.

"He's handsome," Kim said, sipping a glass of well-earned tea.

"Yeah, but that about does it, dearie," Timothy said. Jim appeared out of the restroom. Kim pretended to become busy, while Jim pulled Timothy to the side. Kim beheld the notorious Jim Whaley with intrigue. He was not bad looking at all. She wondered what the problems were between he and ole Norm.

"Hey, who is that?" Jim finally captured enough of Timothy's attention to ask. Jim slightly leaned his head in her direction.

"That ... is Kimberley Brandon, one of Norma's newest and brightest. The camera loves her," Timothy prepared another roll of film. "Now, can I get back to work, sir?" Timothy managed a fake smile. He had no tolerance for Jim Whaley, the biggest mistake that Norma Richmond had ever made, in his assessment!

Jim was too entranced with Kim to pay attention to his sly remarks. He watched the entire session, and was even sober enough to clap at its end. Jim grimaced when Norma entered, right on cue to finishing time.

"So, how did it go, Timothy?" Norma waltzed in smiling. The day's business had gone well for her.

"Great Norma, she's a winner just like you said," Timothy's eyes directed Norma towards her husband, standing aloof.

"Oh, isn't it great to see my hard-working hubby assisting when and where he is needed," Norma snarled with a sarcastic tone. It would be their two-year anniversary in a few days—two years of sheer hell. She would offer him a settlement, since money was all he had been after. She had wanted it to work. Even now as he approached her, she wanted to find reasons to give this marriage a chance.

"Norma, my love, were you not going to introduce me to our newest and brightest model?" Jim's tone was equally as sarcastic.

Timothy quickly gathered his things, as Kim made her way over to be formally introduced.

"Sure, why not? Kimberley Brandon, this is Jim Whaley, my husband. Jim this is Kimberley Brandon," Norma completed her introductions, while Jim hungrily eyed Kim. Kim blushed with embarrassment, and Norma walked away, utterly repulsed. It was as if he had no respect at all anymore, not even for himself. He flirted whenever and wherever he chose.

Timothy Simons cornered Norma, not willing to withstand another minute of Jim's behavior. Timothy whispered loud enough for both Jim and Kimberley to hear, "Norma, I can not understand why a beautiful, intelligent woman such as yourself puts up with this madness. You deserve so much more."

"Thank you for your concern, and thank you for a wonderful session, as always. This one, I will have to handle myself, old friend," Norma was grateful that she had the respect and loyalty of people like Timothy Simons. She welcomed his warm embrace and sweet kiss on the cheek.

"If you need anything at all--" he began.

"I know, and thank you," Norma replied, squeezing his hand. Norma turned to find her husband with his arm around Kim. Kimberley gently pushed Jim away, catching Norma's glance. Right then and there Norma decided that she had had her fill of Jim Whaley for the day.

"Jim, I am returning to my office. You know the number. I don't expect you to wait up. Kim, I will see you first thing tomorrow in my office," Norma walked briskly away.

"What? Wonder what's eating her?" Jim said nonchalantly. Timothy gave him a hateful look and quickly packed his things. The poor bloody bastard really had no clue. Timothy shook his head at him.

"What?" Jim shrugged his shoulders. "Is every one at this place against me?" he said as Kim threw a coy smile his way.

"Well, at least I have one fan," Jim now lustfully eyed Kimberley from head to toe.

Kim examined him closely as well. He really was not half bad. "Would you uh ... like to go somewhere and get a drink?" Jim held out his elbow for her to take.

"Sure, why not?" Kim grabbed his elbow. They marched together towards the outside of the building.

Norma sighed as she made her way out of the photography portion of Ecstacy, and into her own office. Her thoughts consumed her. Why was he always so cruel to her? They could hardly speak anymore without starting an argument. He never made love to her. She could not take him to social events due to his drinking. Where did it all go wrong? What had she said or done to make it go wrong? She was tired of trying to figure it out.

Norma fought the tears, sitting at her desk to finish a light stack of paperwork. It could honestly have waited until the next day. She needed something to give her focus right now. She could not go home right now. She dreaded him being there. She dreaded him *not* being there. The whole office and tabloids discussed his infidelities, drinking, and wild party habits. Her marriage was once again the talk of the town. Everywhere she went, there was whispering behind her back.

Norma blocked it out of her mind and locked it away in her secret place. Work would comfort her now. She picked up the first paper from her stack, and began.

* * *

"So, do you enjoy working for my wife?" Jim said, staring intently and lustfully into Kimberley's luscious green eyes. They had stopped for coffee at a Starbucks on Sunset, not far from the office building.

"Well, I guess you could say that. She is responsible for my success this far," Kim said, staring back just as intently.

"Honey, *you*, with your beautiful self, are responsible for that," Jim dared to put his hand on her chin. Kim did not deny him that. Jim was absolutely entranced by her exotic beauty, her long curly tresses, her shapely body, her angelic face. He had to have her.

"So ... uh ... Miss Brandon," Jim began in a subtle sexy tone.

"Oh, please ... call me Kim," Kim leaned forward a little so he could catch a glimpse of her supple breasts. Jim grinned, his eyes widening with excitement.

"So, Kim, I have seen photographs of you before at my New York office. They hardly do you justice."

Kim raised her eyebrows and smiled. He was fixated on her beauty. That was good. It would make this whole process a lot easier. Kim already had a master plan.

"You know, photography is one of my many hobbies, I would like to take a few photographs of you, myself. That is ... if you wouldn't mind?"

Kim was bored with his senseless chatter.

"Why don't we go some place more private and discuss this," Kim gazed deep into Jim's eyes. Jim looked a little shocked at her forwardness. People in the coffee house were beginning to stare, mainly because they recognized Kim's face.

"Oh hell yeah!" Jim thought, as they made their way to her jeep. She was not going to play coy and hard to get. He liked that in a female. This would be a night to remember.

* * *

Two months later ...

"Uh, uh, uh. Girl, you know you are somethin' fine," Jim stroked his hands up and down Kimberley's smooth, creamy back. They had made their way back to Kim's place for some lovemaking, after a light lunch. Jim smoothed his hand over the satin sheets, and then back to those curly locks on Kim's head.

Jim peered into the face of a woman that finally understood him. They had three very important things in common. They both worshiped money, themselves, and hated Norma Richmond Whaley.

The last two months with her had been a blast. From the moment they had met at that photo session, it was love ... well ... lust at first sight. But twisting his hands through her curly tresses now, Jim knew that it was more than just a 'sex thang.'

So what, had the hustler of all time finally been hustled? Was he really in love or just whipped? He had never met anyone like Kimberley. She was equally as mischievous, exciting, and spontaneous. She was nothing like Norma, neither in mind nor body. He had even stopped drinking for her. Norma had thought it an attempt on his part to make a real change, and make their marriage work. She had even postponed the divorce settlement.

Kim had even convinced Jim to be nicer to Norma, to make her believe their marriage could be salvaged. Staring at this luscious woman at his side, he wanted no part of Norma Richmond Whaley. He wanted out of his loveless, boring marriage.

"What's on your mind, lover?" Kim said, turning to sensuously kiss her lover, while touching and caressing him. She was so glad that he had played right into her hands. Jim was very much a man of his senses, but he also shared some of her own ambitions. They both wanted as much as they could get, and getting *everything* was always a big part of that plan. It took no time at all for Jim to open up about Norma.

Kim soon knew every move that Norma made, thanks to Jim. She had even convinced Jim to have a separate attorney, unknown to Norma, draw up papers that would give him 50% of the profits for all branches of Ecstacy Enterprises should they ever divorce. And of course, she included her own name, in the event that she became the next Mrs. Whaley.

Jim could not believe that Kim had actually got Norma to sign it. Kim explained how she simply mixed it in some papers that Norma was already going to sign. She handed it to Norma, who had had an especially long day. She had already carefully read through the agreement she assumed that she was signing. It was genius. Surely, she would not suspect foul play from a trustworthy and loyal friend. There she was doing double duty, Norma's trusted and loyal employee/friend by day, and worst enemy by night.

Jim had proved a romantic and attentive lover, as well as a terrific partner in crime. He spared no costs when it came to her. He showered her with flowers, bought jewelry, and expensive dinners. He even dipped into some of his own money that he had made from his shoots, as sparse as they had become. He took her to meet in secret out of the way places to make passionate, thrilling love to her. Sometimes they even made love in he and Norma's bed.

A year passed. Kim remained Norma's number one cover girl and most trusted confidant. Money was good now. Kim was now living in Bel Air, driving a Mercedes, dining in exclusive restaurants. She traveled to exotic locations all over the world: Europe, Africa, and Asia. All of the photographers loved and often requested to work with her. Norma even had negotiations under way for a speaking role in a feature film.

Kim was living a dream, but it still was not enough. She was tired of playing up to Norma. She wanted the power all on her own terms. Jim was in heaven, but she definitely wanted more. She wanted to be no one's puppet, and had gathered enough personal and business information to destroy Norma by now. It was time to make a move, time to stop 'jiving' around. It was now time to play hardball.

The Hollywood Hills road turned swiftly underneath Norma's wheels. She passed Hillpark Drive, and failed to slow down at the next yellow street light. She had to hurry. The anonymous note left under her office door warned her to come home immediately. Why? What had Jim done now? Had his drinking finally gotten the best of him? Had he burned down the house? Norma had tried calling, no answer. Her fears intensified.

Norma pulled into the six bedroom, three-story home, to find no lights and no car in sight. All the other houses on their street were lit, and this made everything seem more eerie and dark.

Jim usually left the lights on in the evening, at least. She wondered if there was really something to be concerned about. Fear, guilt, and regret settled in the pit of her stomach, as she hesitantly walked towards the entrance of her door. She remembered her cruel words in the heat of their latest argument, "You're a good for nothing drunk! I hate you! You're nothing to me! I wish you were dead." Boy, she wished she had not said that.

Norma went to unlock her door only to find it already open. She pushed it a little, and then frantically fumbled around in the dark for the gun she had kept in the bottom drawer to defend against prowlers. It was no longer there.

The house felt uneasy under the still, quiet dark. Norma switched on all the lights she could find and yelled out, "Jim! Jim!" No answer, only silence.

Norma noticed overturned bottles and a broken lamp in the middle of the living room floor. Her eyes widened in horror, as she noticed a bright red spot on the carpet. It looked like blood. Maybe it was Jim's blood ... Norma knelt down to examine it, "Oh, God," Norma said, sobbing and swallowing hard, "Jim!

Jim!" she screamed at the top of her lungs. Still, no response. Norma's heart pounded in her chest.

Norma quickly ascended up the first set of stairs turning on each light she came into contact with. She then kept running until she had reached the end of the final stairway. She noticed a glowing light coming from her guest bedroom. Norma sighed with relief.

Maybe he was all right after all. Maybe he just tripped and cut himself. What would make him stop this drinking? She had even deduced the mysterious note to a concerned neighbor who was worried, because of the noise that he was making. By the time Norma reached the bedroom door, she had a few more angry words for Jim Whaley. She had left a stack of important paper on her desk for this!

Norma opened her bedroom door, her mouth flew open in shock. There was her husband, reclined on his back, completely naked, huffing and puffing as some scantily clad tramp rode him as if he were a rodeo horse. The nerve of this man! How could he do this in their home?

"Aw, aw baby," Jim moaned in obvious pleasure as the woman began grinding him faster. Norma looked over at the television, which had obviously provided the glow from outside of the room. She switched it off, and looked up to stare at a humiliated Jim.

"I didn't ... real ... didn't know you were coming home this early," Jim managed, curdling the covers around his waist and getting up to explain. Norma had lost interest in his words. The mysterious woman clad in red lingerie, loosed her long wavy hair from her short bobbed wig. Norma stared into the face of the woman she had considered a dear friend up to this point.

Kimberley Brandon faced her new opponent with pride, her soulless eyes oozing with unspeakable hatred.

"Why Kim? Why this? You could have ... have any man ... any man you ... you want ... why?" Norma could hardly get her words out. "He's only ... only using you. He will be on to the next one after you ... I made you what you are! Why ... why betray me this way?" a tear trickling down her face. It was only a matter of time before Jim had betrayed her in such a way, but Kim ... not Kim. Norma hurried out of the room, Jim following at her heels.

"Baby, why don't you just let me explain, I ... I ... " Jim stammered.

Norma stopped at the top of the stairs. Never turning to face him, she spoke once more, "Jim, I want a divorce. Pack your shit and get out! I don't want you and that tramp here when I get back!"

Jim continued to plead for her forgiveness, as Norma scurried down the last flight of stairs. He followed her to the bottom of the stairs to no avail. It was no use. With a deaf ear, she had opened and slammed the front door without acknowledging another word. Jim stood staring at the front door, as if he were waiting for her to return.

Kim descended slowly and calmly, unscathed by all that had occurred.

"What am I supposed to do? She will ruin us both, " Jim complained. Kim stood ready to console him. Jim looked at his beautiful mistress, sweat still glistening on her light brown skin from their recent encounter. Jim stood with tears in his eyes, the covers still curdled around his waist. Kim said nothing, preferring to answer him only with a hungry, sensual kiss. They kissed, making their way back to the bedroom to make love once more.

Chapter
<u>8</u>

The Guiding Light

Norma would have normally gone back to the office to work off her frustration, but for once she had no strength to make it there. Her eyes were blurry and her head felt light from all of the crying. She pulled into a nightclub not far from her Hollywood hills home.

Norma entered as the music drummed out, "Love like this before," Faith Evans sang as women scantily clad and men with bulging eyeballs seemed to appear from every direction. Norma took a seat at the bar, and asked for a Martini on the rocks. Norma was not a heavy drinker, but she needed something different tonight. She needed something to numb the pain a little. She did not want to think, at least, not until tomorrow.

About a dozen people must have come up to her to ask for her autograph within the first hour. One man bought her a drink, and at least three tried to pick her up. Finally, a man that looked as if he were in his mid forties settled in a seat next to hers.

He was clean-shaven, suit and tie, nice, short cut hair. He looked decent enough. Norma could tell from the look in his eye that he recognized her, but he was trying not to let on.

"Hello," he said after ordering vodka.

Norma was in no mood for anymore pick ups tonight, but she still decided to be cordial. "Hello, yourself," she said with a quick smile, then turned away.

"Can I buy you another drink?" he said, ignoring her cold shoulder routine.

"No, I think I am just about done here," Norma held up her drink to toast at him. She then realized that this was her third drink. She frowned at the drink.

"Is there something wrong?" he noted her strange frown.

"Oh, no I just noticed, I ... oh, never mind," Norma placed her hand over her head.

"May I ask what a beautiful lady like you is doing in a place like this?" he gently touched his moustache lifting his thick eyebrows.

"Is there somewhere else I am supposed to be?" Norma was a little sarcastic. It finally started to kick in, that weird sensation. Norma had not been drunk since the first night she got the news that she was going to be the cover for *Essence*. That was at least twelve years ago. Norma finished her drink and tipped the glass towards the bartender, "Bottoms up," Norma said to the gentleman next to her, who watched as she stumbled out of her chair.

"Oh, careful, or you'll hurt yourself," he rose up out of his chair to catch her fall.

Norma snatched her arm away. Why would he not just leave her alone! She was tired of him by now. She was tired of all men! Everyone just wanted a piece of her as if she were some damn cake. No one wanted her for the person she was. She had worked so hard to be useful and independent, but now she just felt vulnerable and small.

"No, I can do it my ... myself!" she said a little too loudly.

Everyone turned in their direction to see what was going on. The man fixed his collar, checked around to see who was watching, and walked away. Sure, she was a celebrity and everything, but what gave her the right to talk to a person like that!

"That's right, walk away! They all do!" Tears began to form in the corner of her eyes. The manager appeared to see what everyone was gawking at. She no longer cared. She just had to get away. This whole thing had been a terrible idea.

Norma stumbled her way through the parking lot until she finally reached her car. She climbed in and got on her back seat. She looked at her watch.

It was 2:30 a.m. "I'll sleep it off, and then I'll go home," Norma mumbled, reclining in her back seat. Sleep began to take over in no time.

Norma wrestled in her sleep, no peace in her rest. First, she imagined a funny colored lion, not the coppery yellow or brown like normal, but wine red. The lion eyed her curiously, never bothering even to roar. Norma could see herself as a child in the dream, pigtails and all. She scurried away from the lion, leading her down a warm, sunny path, paved with green and russet colored rocks. The pathway made its end at a rainbow covered waterfall.

Norma marveled, looking up at the beautiful waterfall. She yearned to taste the coolness of its soothing waters. Suddenly, a huge roar drowned out the beauty of her surroundings. Norma jerked her body to view an eight foot, huge, silvery bear clawing at her. Norma screamed in terror, but somehow, she could hear a calming voice calling to her in the near distance.

Norma was awakened by a tap on her car window. It was the police. Norma eyed her watch. Now, it was 6:30 the next morning. The sun of a new day was making its way on the Los Angeles horizon. Norma could hear the sounds of pigeons nestling outside her car door.

"Ma'am, we noticed your car parked. We ran the license plate. Wow, I can not believe it's really you," the officer said, as Norma tried to pull up her heavy aching head to roll down the window.

"Sir, I ..." Norma began.

"Well, just be careful Miss Richmond. It's not safe to park at a place like this all night. Have a safe rest of the day," he said, seeing that she was in no mood to respond to a doting fan.

"Yes," Norma nodded her head and sighing in relief, as he walked away. She grimaced, as she vaguely recalled the awful scene she had made in the bar the night before. She wished there was some way she could apologize to the poor gentleman she had exploded all of her anger upon. He had not deserved that.

And then, Norma began to recall everything that had led her to being in the back of her own car. All of the events of the past evening flashed before her eyes, replaying again and again. All of the pain returned, as if it had never left. Now she felt even worse than before.

Suddenly, a sound emerged from her own throat, seemingly from the bottom of her soul. Norma could not recognize her own voice crying out. She felt such immeasurable pain, such feelings of rejection, and loneliness. She felt so used. How could any man make her feel this way?

And then it finally happened. Norma bowed her head in the leather interior of her car, and began to weep and weep ... and weep. She finally managed to cry out, "O God, oh ... God I'm so sorry oh please help me! I know that I have wandered away from you and the teachings my mother gave me so long ago, but I know that you can help me!"

She paused for a moment, as a quiet, still thought entered her mind. Norma looked up towards the sky and said aloud, "Thank you, God, I know the answer now. I can still find a way to call home." With that said, Norma reached over her front seat to look in her glove compartment. She pulled out her cell phone to dial her sister, Juanita.

The phone rang three times, and then her sister mumbled a groggy hello from across the world.

"Sis, it's Norma," she said, grateful that she had answered.

"Yeah girl, what's all that noise, girl?" Juanita said, lowering her voice, seeming to detect the sorrow in Norma's voice already.

Without hesitation the words came out, "Can you get here, Nita? I will send for you. I need you." Norma now sounded much like the youngest rather than the oldest. She so needed family now.

"Yes, you know I will, what is it Norma?" Juanita said, now fully awake.

"It's Jim. I caught him with my best model ... someone that I *thought* was my friend in my ...." Norma began.

"Say no more, I am on my way. Call you when I get in," Juanita said as Norma let out an exasperating sigh.

By this time, Juanita had awakened her husband. Larry Jenkins was all too curious as to why his wife was taking clothes out of her closet on this Saturday morning. Juanita hugged him and gave a subtle morning kiss, remembering when Norma had asked her if she was "really serious about this one". The questioning look in his eyes sent her into a flurry of explanations. "Honey, that jerk has finally done it this time. He will not hurt my sister anymore. You just don't understand. She needs me right now, Larry, and ..." Juanita ranted on as he rubbed her back in comfort.

"Wooh wooh, slow it down. What are you talking about?" Larry said, now affectionately cuddling her to his body to calm her.

"It's Norma. She finally caught him with his pants down, literally," Juanita now gathering socks, stockings, and underwear from her drawers.

"But honey, what are you gonna do bout' it? What about your patients? Norma is a big girl ..."

"Sweetheart, you don't understand. She's my sister, and she needs me right now. That's all that matters. Can you handle half of my load for the week? I will cancel the rest from Los Angeles," she gazed deeply into his eyes for support and approval. They shared a small, but fruitful practice in the center of town. Virginian life had proved quiet, but challenging enough for her taste. They had a good life, and a solid marriage.

Juanita hated putting off responsibilities on her husband. She would not ask or expect of him what she would not be willing to reciprocate. She needed him to say it was okay.

"Baby, that's no problem. My concern is, can *you* handle all of this in *your* condition?" Larry was referring to the pregnancy they had just recently learned about. They had been married a year now, and were both anxiously awaiting their first baby.

"I was raised a Richmond. I can do anything," Juanita said, pulling her suitcase from the closet. The "I am woman" look on her face convinced her husband that there was no use trying to convince her otherwise. He reluctantly helped his wife pack, and made the reservations.

Norma arrived home to an empty house with a throbbing headache from her slight hangover. Jim had packed all of his things and gone during the night. She wandered aimlessly through her house from bedroom to bedroom like a zombie, numb from too much spent emotion. Each room brought out a new and painful memory for her, some were pleasant, especially of the first days she and Jim had shared in their home. This newest betrayal came as no big shock, at least not on Jim's part. Maybe she would sell the house.

It all seemed like a horrible nightmare from which she could not awake. Her mind fixated on Kim's hateful look. It was like she had been proud of what she had done. That tramp! How could she betray her like this? After all that she had done for her. She had shared secrets with her, personal and business information. She had opened up the world of modeling to her, and trusted her as a friend.

Kim had never seemed threatened by her authority and power. She had soaked up information like a sponge, and proved a worthy student. Norma had watched for those common signs of envy and jealousy. She had misjudged her character in every way.

Well, it was over now. Norma would demand Kim's resignation from Ecstacy as soon as she returned. Her career would be over as quick as it had begun. Everyone knew that if

Norma let you go, it was for a good reason. It was like being blacklisted. No one would touch her.

Norma thought back to the letter that had sent her to this misfortune. Had Kim sent that letter, somehow? Did she want to hurt her that bad? What had she done to deserve this? She reflected back to the cold look in Kim's eyes, such hatred and malice. It sent a chill through her body to think of it now. Kim's hatred was now all too apparent, but Norma had no clue as to what that was all about.

Norma remembered Sable's fateful words that day she had been thwarted from Ecstacy, "She is a she-wolf, and she will betray you. Mark my words," she had warned. How right she had been.

Norma collapsed on her couch to rest, and focused on the phone. She hoped Juanita would call soon to say she had arrived. She hurt so much inside that she thought she would bleed. The tears now riveted freely down her beautiful brown face, faster than she could wipe them away.

How could she pull herself back together again? How could she draw her soul out of this deep dark well, and into the light again?

She would put in a call to Brookton, and other loyal business partners in the city. The affairs of Ecstacy would be left to them until she could return at full force.

Norma walked slowly over to her kitchen. She turned the knob on her gas stove and grabbed her silver tea pot. Norma looked nervously at the phone. She placed the teapot on the stove, anxiously awaiting her sister's call.

Jim and Kimberley sat on Kim's black leather couch, Jim confessing his love.

"I don't care what has happened. I just want to be with you," Jim said, stroking Kim's beautiful tresses.

"But Jim, you *are* still married. If you think that I am going to continue to be your mistress, well ..." Kim turned up her nose and walked away from Jim.

Jim grabbed her from behind and held her close, "Baby, as soon as the divorce is final, I promise that I will marry you."

Kim took a deep breath as she recalled Norma's words, "He's just using you .... He'll be on to the next ...." She would prove her wrong.

"Do you really mean that?" Kim said, turning to look at his sad eyes.

"Yes baby, I really mean that. I love you," Jim sincerely embraced the woman that he truly loved.

"But Norma is going to kick me straight out of Ecstacy. I will be history by the time she gets through ..." Kim began.

"All of that will be settled as soon as *you* are my wife. Remember, the document that you got her to sign. We will own 50% of Norma's company, together baby, and it's all because of you," Jim kissed her softly on the head and reassured her with his eyes.

Kim smiled, finally content that her plan was working. "Yeah, it will all work out just fine, just like I planned," Kim thought to herself. Jim held on to her for dear life.

Norma scuffled around a crowded L.A.X. Airport searching for her sister that evening. All she had to see was that haircut, and she would know it was her from miles away. Norma compulsively checked her watch. Should she ask the attendant *again* about the flight?

"Norma Jeanette," Juanita said, sneaking up behind her sister who had been pacing from the gateway to the coffee shop for the last twenty minutes.

"Hey, Nita," Norma was grateful to hear her voice and see her face again.

"Oh, I forgot to tell you before you even start, I'm about two months pregnant. You are gonna be an auntie," Juanita gleamed with joy. Norma laughed and embraced the sister she so adored.

"Oh, I am so happy for you and Larry, I ..." Norma began, her sister scowling and drawing back her chin.

"Girl, you look like hell! You never finished telling me what happened," Norma lifted the bag from her sister's hands, accompanied her to the baggage claim area.

"Gee thanks sis," Norma said with a sheepish grin, "As I told you, I caught him with my best model and girlfriend, but that was not the worst part. It was in my house ... in my guest bed." Norma held her mouth and blinked away the surfacing tears. She did not want to start the crying again.

"Oh nah girl," Juanita paused, speechless for a moment. "Well Norma girl, I hate to say I told you so ..." Juanita began.

"Then don't," Norma said as their eyes met and locked. Her sister nodded in understanding.

The two sisters talked and reminisced on old times from the airport to the house. Juanita's mouth sprang open when they pulled into Norma's three-story, six-bedroom home in the Hollywood Hills.

"So this is how you movie stars live, hot dog it!" Juanita glided up the driveway and opening the door to the most beautiful house she had ever seen.

Norma had bought this house specifically for when she and Jim married. It had been her dream house. The home where she had lived before was about fifteen miles away, closer to Silver Lake. It was modest compared to this place.

The doorway opened to a large oriental style rug draped across the plush white carpets cleaned not a month ago. Juanita dropped her bags at the door and opened her mouth. She walked in amazement from one room to the next. The walls complemented the rugs with its soft creamy colored hue.

Large portraits of Norma and other now famous models (made so by Ecstacy) provided decoration for the downstairs living room, dining room and office space of Norma's home.

The spacious kitchen and downstairs bathroom were set in shiny black marble. Juanita could see her own reflection in the immaculately clean marble. The gas stove looked barely used. Marie would be happy at how clean the place had been kept.

"You clean this place yourself?" Juanita remembered her sister's creative mind, but not so clean room at their old home. Norma was one for directing others how to clean, rather than cleaning herself.

"I hire a maid service to come in once every two weeks, and I help them clean," Norma admitted.

Juanita nodded, she could still see Norma directing folks where and when to clean. She laughed a little to herself.

The living room reminded Juanita of the old Southern style furniture of her past. The living room was spacious, with a large couch settled at its middle. The couch was white, with subtle floral designs, covered to preserve and protect its beauty.

The fireplace provided for a romantic setting in the middle of the room. The thirty-six inch wide screen television set resting in the front of the couch, would have been her husband's fondest dream come true. Juanita smiled to herself.

The modest dining room set was subtle and classy in style, as any dining room in the traditional south. There was a setting for six, tablecloths, silverware, candelabra and all.

Juanita suddenly remembered the rich white folks. It was a bit eerie how similar Norma's living and dining room furniture was to those old Virginian homes.

Juanita had cleaned a few of those homes to help put herself through college. This brought back many bittersweet memories.

Instead of a traditional backyard, Norma's back screen opened to an indoor shower, sauna and swimming pool. Jim's heavyweights lay by the pool, beginning to collect rust. Norma gasped a little. She had forgotten that Jim had left it there.

"See, we still had space for a mini-backyard," Norma quickly led her sister out of the room where Jim's presence still lingered. Upon exiting this additional room, one could still enjoy a small yard with wild flowers. There was an orange tree blooming in the midst. The room occupied most of the space. Juanita noted that she would remember to gather some oranges to take home.

Juanita stepped back inside the house. There was still so much to see. She made her way to a locked cabinet in a secluded hallway, next to the kitchen. Juanita marveled at its contents.

Norma had encased a contemporary collection of black sculptures, antique silver tea cups, wineglasses, plates, at least three beautifully embroidered china sets, and a few pieces of crystal.

It was all ever so reminiscent of Mama. Juanita reflected on her mama's bright smile and beautiful face. This cabinet, with all its unique treasures. It was exactly the way mama would have done it, even down to the way it had been ordered and arranged.

Juanita paused for a moment, her southern roots and past combining and somehow being made new. She felt a deep sense of pride, delighted by the ease with which Norma had put it all together. Norma had put much thought into every crevice of design in this house.

Juanita noticed a cup sitting next to the kitchen sink, which reminded her of one her mother had, "Where on earth did you find this?"

"If you search hard enough you can find anything in L.A.," Norma said, delighted at her sister's surprised look. "Let me give you the rest of the grand tour," Norma said, leading her sister up the churrigueresque style rail which winded up in spiral fashion from one story to the next of the three-story home.

Paintings by new contemporary black artists loomed the walls leading to each story, along with copies of original famous paintings by artists such as: Aaron Douglas, Archibald Motley, and William Johnson. Norma had arrived, and Juanita was proud.

A twinge of jealousy surged through Juanita as she stepped from the hall, and entered her sister's huge master bedroom. There was a king size bed, spacious walk-in closet, vanity set complete with a large mirror, accessories, and golden brush.

The bathroom attached was quite large as well. Juanita saw the bathtub, which she could have easily mistaken for a jacuzzi. Beside the bathtub, there was a small shower, with opaque, clear glass. There was a separate door which led to the toilet inside. Juanita marveled at the grandiosity of her sister's living.

Her modest Virginian home, which had been considered exquisite in its own right, seemed cottage-like in comparison. Norma could not help but notice the look on her sister's face.

"So, you want it? You can have for about ten bucks," Norma forced a laugh, quickly shifting into a whimper, and finally a cry. The tears began to flow again, as if somebody had unstopped the dam. Juanita just held and rocked her, and allowed her to cry. She held her sister, guilty that she had felt even a hint of envy. After all, Norma had worked so hard, and deserved everything she had worked for. Besides, her own house was beautiful, and she had more than everything that she needed.

"Mama would sure be proud of you, Norma. This is truly a dream house fit for a queen. You are a queen, remember that, baby girl. You just have not found the right king yet," Juanita said in a soft voice.

"Yeah, but looks like my dream has become a nightmare. And looks like I'm gonna be sitting on this here throne all by myself. Nita, what am I gonna do?" Norma asked rhetorically. Her sister held her a little bit tighter.

"Why don't you stop trying so hard and just let me do everything for a while," Juanita implored. Norma finally let go of Juanita, nodding her head in agreement.

"But the baby ..." Norma began, concerned for Juanita's health.

"For once, why don't you let someone take care of you. Let me be the big sister for a change," Juanita held Norma's head to her breast. This reminded Norma of her mother. Juanita would make this child such a great mother. Juanita was right. Maybe she would let someone else tell her what to do for a while.

Norma showed her sister in to the guest room next to what Norma now called the "room-of-doom." It was equally as beautiful, but a bit smaller. There was another bathroom just down the hall. It would be like old times, her sister a bedroom away from her own.

Norma sighed a little, "Wanted to fill this house with a few kids, you know. Maybe I'll never get the chance, now."

Juanita could see that it would take much time for her to get past her pain and anger. She would be there to get her through the worst of it, but she would have to do most of the work herself.

"Night, Nita. I am so glad you're here," Norma hugged her one last time before she entered her room.

"Night Norma Jeanette, sleep tight. I'll be just down the hall if you need me ... just like old times," Juanita watched her sister walk down the hall to retire for the evening.

Juanita was truly heaven sent for Norma. For the entire week, she insisted on cooking, washing, helping the maid service clean, and taking all of Norma's messages. The only thing that *she* insisted, was that Norma take her to a church that Sunday. Norma had not been to church in ages, and she enjoyed the service.

Juanita had stuck to her traditional southern roots and upbringing. Juanita would get up and pray every morning, sing hymns as she did chores, and almost preach the gospel, just like Mama. Norma admired her sense of spirituality. She and her husband usually attended church every Sunday, and Juanita was always encouraging her more worldly sister to attend. Norma observed her sister's solid composure and strong character, and thought "maybe she's got something I am missing."

Norma remembered how vulnerable she had been that moment in the car. A small voice seemed to guide her to call her sister that day. Funny, she had always pictured herself as the strong one. Juanita was her stronghold now.

Juanita waited on Norma hand and foot, even though *she* was the one pregnant. Juanita claimed that it was good therapy for the both of them. Norma stopped fussing after a while, and enjoyed it. She knew that it was what she needed, and Marie would have wanted them to see about one another.

Juanita put in a few calls to her poor husband, who missed her terribly after the first week. His concern for her and their child intensified when Norma asked her to stay just one more week. Norma envied her sister, Jim had not cared where she went, much less how long she was gone. It hurt to realize that he probably never loved her at all. He had only wanted the money. That was all.

"What? Baby I can not believe this! You said *one* week. One week! When are you coming home, baby? I need you too," Larry sounded frustrated and lonely. Not to mention, her load of patients were piling on his back. He needed and loved her so much.

"Soon, I just have to help her through this ... understand ... just *one* more week," Juanita looked at her sister still sulking in front of the television.

Juanita quickly hung up from her husband, took a deep breath, and picked up the receiver. She peeped out at Norma, making sure that she was not paying close attention. Juanita dialed fast. She did not want to lose her nerve. The phone rang three times, then, the voice of her baby sister resonated in her ears.

"Flora, there is someone that you need to speak to. I think that it's a good time for you to resolve some things," Juanita whispered into the phone.

"Yeah, Nita, but ..." Flora began, but stopped when she realized her sister had already left the phone.

Juanita explained to Norma that it was an important phone call. She put the phone in Norma's face, and retreated behind the stairs.

Flora had recognized her sister's voice, but had no idea what she was talking about. When she heard Norma's grouchy voice, she almost hung up. Why did Nita do this? Norma was the one that needed to apologize for all of those horrible things she had said at the funeral. Imagine ... blaming her for Marie's death. It was her mother too. Nobody was to blame.

"Hello, Norma. It's good tah hear yor' voice," Flora said, her accent oozing out at every other word.

Norma was too tired to fight, and it was too late to hang up now. Norma turned to give her sister an evil look. Juanita had hidden behind the first two steps, and was now peeking out to supervise the conversation.

"Hello, Flora. It's really good to hear your voice, too. It has really been a long time."

Juanita watched from the stairway, as Norma amazingly continued responding and talking. Juanita waited for maybe, ten minutes, but it seemed like a whole hour. Norma's laughter roared and echoed from the living room. Juanita felt that it was safe to come out and sit beside her sister, who willingly allowed her to hold her hand. She squeezed her hand back, and smiled to let her know that it was all right. Boy, had she mellowed. There would have been a time, when the mention of Flora's name would have sparked a large controversy.

Norma began frantically nodding her head in agreement with something that Flora was saying. Juanita kept trying to catch Norma's attention, and mouthing "What?" so that she could give her some idea of what she was saying. Norma just stared at Juanita, tears beginning to well up in her eyes. One tear descended down her cheek successfully.

Juanita's curiosity was too much for her to bear, so she decided to wander over, and grab the kitchen phone. Juanita was surprised to hear Flora, way across the world, crying as well, "I'm sorry ... if you fe ... felt I kept somethin' from yah ... it wasn't my fault. She was ... she was my momma, too. She made me promise hur ... I swear it. She tol' me not to say nothin'. By tha time I did, it was too late. I shoulda said somethin', I just swore I was'nt gonna. I am sooo sorry," she said, her voice finally breaking up and wailing. Juanita started crying as well now.

"You are right. It was not all you, baby sis. It was me, too. I should never have blamed you ... it's just that I lo ... I loved her so much," Norma now fiddled her hair with her fingers, crying as well, "And I love you, too. Marie would never have wanted us to feud like this," Norma glanced over at her beloved sister, wailing in the kitchen corner. They were all crying now. In that moment it all seemed to flash back, the funeral, the arguments, the hurt. Now, the reason why they had separated, would now bring them together again—Marie. Only *she* could do that.

Juanita broke the silence, "I wish you were here so we could all have a group hug." They all broke into laughter. "I am so glad we had dis' talk, Norm, Please come visit soon." Flora was relieved that the hatchet was finally put to rest. Eight years was too long to fight. They had missed out on too much. It was as if she had lost them both, her mother and oldest sister.

"No, *you* come out here and visit me. And how are my two nieces, and that husband of yours?" a smile of release and relief rested on Norma's tear-streaked face. She had missed out on so much. They would have to make up for lost time.

"Fine, and what about you? Juanita told me that you got hitched," Flora said.

"Whoops," Juanita butt in, "fill you in on the rest when I get home, Flor."

Flora took that as a cue to exit, before she created any new damage, "Well, I guess I'll talk to yah both later. Call me sometime, Norm."

"I will, my little southern flower," Norma repeated their mother's favorite pet name for her sister.

"Goodbye, now."

"Goodbye," Norma said as all three of them hung up the phone together. Norma rushed over to her sister and held on for dear life.

"Thank you, sis, not only for that, but for everything." They embraced and settled in front of the television.

Norma decided to take the rest of the week to show her sister around. It was much harder for Juanita to convince her worried husband that it would only be five more days. After all, there were patients to consider. She was already a week behind schedule.

For the next five days, Norma and Juanita had the time of their lives. They journeyed to Universal City Walk, the Chinese Mann Theater, Wax Museum, and a few fancy restaurants around Beverly Hills and Hollywood.

Norma introduced Nita to some of her famous entertainer and actor friends, in town for film and video shoots—Denzel Washington, Rita Moreno, Patti Labelle, and Nick Nolte. They even caught "Phantom of the Opera", before it made its final run in the Los Angeles area. Juanita even got the chance to meet the famous, Michael Crawford.

Juanita was "celebrity-ed" out by the end of the week. It was time to get back to her practice, and to the love of her life. She knew that Norma would be strong enough to endure, whatever the storm.

Friday morning found Norma and Juanita at the ever so busy L.A.X. Airport. They stood at Juanita's gateway, stammering for finalizing words, the stewardess made the first boarding call.

"Well, here we are again," Juanita was teary eyed but smiling.

"Yeah," Norma searched for the words. How would she face the world alone. For these two weeks, her sister had been there to stop every painful tear from falling. She had seen her through the worst of it. Now, it was time to face the cold, cruel world again.

"I guess that's me. I love you big sis," Juanita said, embracing Norma for the last time. "Promise me, that if I ever need it, you will do the same for me."

"Sure, you know I will, but I really don't think you will need it," Norma's heart jumped a little. She wished there was someone as loving and concerned waiting home for her. Larry Jenkins had faithfully called every night.

"Is my wife ever coming home?" Larry had whimpered. Norma remembered fearing him half-serious.

"I love you. Now get your butt on that plane, Mrs. Jenkins," she watched her turn and walk away. Her eyes followed her until she disappeared with the rest of the passengers.

Norma stayed until the Delta Airlines flight lifted off, taking her sister back halfway across the world. She had been like Humpty Dumpty. Juanita had been there to pick up the shattered pieces, and put her back together again. She had been much like a guiding light on a stormy, dark night. She was even considering returning to the church they had attended last Sunday.

Norma noticed how cloudy the sky was beginning to look on this cold winter evening. It looked as if it were going to rain. It was early March. It would soon be spring again. Funny, how it would all end in the season that it had begun. This marriage should never have happened.

Norma's mind turned back to work, as the 101 freeway signs indicated that she was nearing her home. She was interested in seeing how they had gotten along without her. It had been two weeks. They must have thought she was dead by now. She would call Brookton and all of her associates, and tell them she was returning early Monday morning. Work never bothered her. She would be back in sync, as soon as she stepped in her office.

Norma sighed, pondering the future havoc that her two biggest enemies would cause—Kimberley Brandon and Jim Whaley. She knew that they were probably somewhere together. The thought of it sickened her stomach. She wondered what would be their next move. Whatever it was, she would be ready for them.

Chapter
<u>9</u>

Papers

"I hereby declare Jim and Norma Richmond Whaley legally divorced on the grounds of irreconcilable differences," the judge proclaimed. Kim and Norma viciously eyed one another. Kim grabbed Jim's hand, and finally rolled her eyes away. Eight months of bitter arguments and malicious slander, would finally be put to rest.

"Jim Whaley, you are obligated to pay alimony to your ex-wife on a monthly basis. This should in some way recompense for the items that you charged to your wife's credit during the marriage. Should you fail to meet the payments in a timely manner, action from this court will be taken against you," the judge glared up at Jim, placing her glasses on her nose.

The judge then continued, "Now, concerning the signed document, allotting 50% of profits from income of Norma Richmond-Whaley's modeling agency to Mr. Whaley, in the event of a divorce. The court recognizes the circumstances under which this signature was obtained. I have taken this under serious consideration, Mrs. Whaley. However, this is a legal, binding document drawn up by a legal attorney. I admonish you to be more cautious of what documents you sign from now on."

Norma looked to her attorney as the judge continued, "I will not award the full 50% in this agreement, considering Mr. Whaley's infidelity, and obvious intentions to gain financially from this marriage." Norma sighed with relief.

"I will, however, award 30% of profit shares for *one* of the Ecstacy branches, provided that Norma Richmond-Whaley, be given the choice of which branch Jim Whaley serves in the capacity rendered by his former wife," the judge ordered. Norma's heart sank.

"There will be a new contractual agreement drawn between the two acting attorneys stating the terms of the new agreement. Should there be any breach in contract, and if Mr. Whaley in any way dishonors his part of this agreement, it will be rendered null and void. Is that understood Mr. Whaley?" the judge inquired. Jim nodded in agreement.

"Yes, ma'am," he replied, hugging an all too content Kimberley.

"This court is adjourned!" the judge declared, rising from her seat.

"I am so sorry. I know that you don't want that jerk to get ..." Norma's lawyer began. But Norma had already made her way over to Jim and Kimberley. Kim stood up glaring at Norma, daring her to speak with her devilish stare. Norma walked slowly over to Kim, looking from her to Jim.

"Norma, I ..." a guilt- ridden Jim began.

Norma slapped Kim hard, as the bailiff, and lawyer rushed to get hold of her. Oohs and ahs sounded all across the courtroom. Jim gently held his new fiancé by the arm and escorted her out of the courtroom.

"This isn't over, Kim!" Norma yelled at Kim. Norma's lawyer advised her to quiet down. The courtroom and press went into a frenzy. Norma knew how bad it looked, but this time she did not care. Kim had nerve to show her face today. It was bad enough that she had had to fire her in person.

Kim never turned her head, but muttered quietly under her breath, upon exiting the courtroom—Jim at her side, "No, Norma, you're right. It's really just beginning."

* * *

Later that weekend in Las Vegas ...

"And I now pronounce you husband and wife," the minister announced to the couple, "You may kiss the bride."

Jim hungrily grabbed his new bride, kissing her with fervent passion, then embracing her tightly. Kim stared into space, her new husband caressing her gently.

This was not the way she had imagined it. She had wanted the white gown, bridesmaids, the big reception. She felt so cheated. This was all Norma's fault.

Kim rudely snatched her bouquet from the girl that she had asked to witness their wedding, and headed towards the center of the hotel. She closed her eyes, imagining family and friends at every side, smiling at her achievement, yelling congratulations.

"What's wrong Kim?" Jim was concerned that his bride did not seem quite as ecstatic. She looked so magnificent in her soft pink gown, carnations flowing in her beautiful hair. He licked his lips and smiled.

"Nothing, honey, I just ... I just wanted to invite some of our friends, I just ... " Kim began.

"Listen, if you come upstairs with me to the room, I will make all of your worries disappear," Jim picked her up in the middle of the casino and carried her to the elevator. Kim's vibrant laughter had many guests in the casino lounge inquiring about the couple. The elevator opened, as Kim kicked, screamed and laughed vivaciously.

"You mean there is nothing that we can do to contest this, Jon," Norma said, pacing back and forth in her lawyer's office.

"Norma, the judge tried to be as fair as she ..." Jonathon began.

"Fair! Giving that creep an inch of what I BUILT is not fair," Norma's cheeks seemed to swell from her anger.

"Norma, its a legal, contractual agreement, with your signature and date. It would be in your best interest to help me draw up a new agreement that solidifies the judges instructions," Jon explained. Norma finally plopped down in a chair in front of his desk

Jonathon Newman had been Norma's attorney since she had moved to Los Angeles. He was a forty-two year old tall, handsome man, with sultry dark brown hair, eyes and smooth skin. His strong muscular body, and clean-shaven look had attracted many women in his "player days".

Jonathon Newman was a changed man now. He now had a well-earned reputation as a respectable attorney. He was a man of decency, integrity, and honesty. He handled mostly entertainment law, contract negotiations, lawsuits when needed, corporate contracts, etc. He had been handling all of Norma's attorney related needs, since she had arrived in Los Angeles. They had been introduced by her longtime business partner, Charles Brookton. Like everyone else, he had warned Norma against marrying Jim, but opted to draw her up the prenuptial agreement when she would not relent. He knew that Jim was scum from the start. He hated to see a woman that he so admired be deceived. Jim had no idea how to treat such a classy, beautiful woman like Norma. "And she is *all* woman," Jonathon thought to himself, smiling as he scanned her side profile from top to bottom.

Norma stood thinking pensively about her next move. She loved her company too much to share it with that ... that ... dog!

"Have you spoken with Jim's lawyer?" Norma turned to face him. Jon cleared his throat to catch his train of thought, "Yes, I have. He said that Jim had him draw up the documents with the belief that it was what you both wanted."

"I cannot believe that bastard! How could he do this?" Norma said, slamming her hand against his desk. Jon was shocked. He never wanted to get on her bad side.

"Oh, I'm sorry," Norma apologized for pounding on his desk.

"Look, Norma I know that you don't want to think about this, but I might as well ask you about it now. Have you decided which branch you would prefer Jim take profits and have some executive control?" Jon braced himself for her next reaction. He had never seen her lose so much of her cool grace and composure. It was strange. It made her seem so vulnerable, even more appealing in a way. He wanted to take her and hold her in his arms. He wanted to protect her from all of this pain.

Norma shook her head and waved her arms out, "No, I can't decide that right now, Jon. That's too much. I can't handle it."

Jon could no longer fight the urge to physically calm her, "Okay, okay, calm down," Jon caressed her arms and smoothed his thumbs across her skin gently. Norma backed away a little. That felt nice, a little too nice.

"Enough of this. Why don't we go out to lunch. It will take your mind off of things. Hey, I'll even treat, and you won't even have to pay for this session," Jon said smiling.

Norma smiled a little surprised. Was he *on* something today? Jonathon Newman was an excellent attorney. He earned and expected his pay.

"So, what's the occasion, Mr. Newman?" Norma anxiously awaited his response. After all, he was a famous attorney. He had a very busy schedule. He had even offered to treat her.

"To see a smile on that beautiful face of yours. So, so what do you say?" Jon said, not trying to hide his look of anticipation.

"Why not?" Norma took his hand. They marched out of his office like debutantes.

"Cancel all of my appointments for the rest of the day," Jon called out to his secretary, as they made their way out of the office and on to the hall.

Kim lay on her back, staring at her reflection in the ceiling mirror of their hotel room. It had been an intense night of lovemaking for them, and Kim guessed that it was probably well after noon by now. She looked over at her husband, who had fallen asleep with a content look on his face. He was now snoring and lay helplessly on his stomach.

Kim finally decided to get up and go to the balcony which overlooked a gorgeous view of the Las Vegas Strip. People scurried back and forth on the streets to whatever destination. They were staying at the Egyptian style hotel, Luxor. Kim could see the MGM, Excalibur, and New York hotels from either direction she turned.

Kim felt as if she were Cleopatra, swept away in her palace, her beloved Mark Antony at her side. Now, they would conquer the world together.

The afternoon heat was already beginning to surface, as gamblers and tourists made their way in and out of each hotel. Maybe she would order up some room service. Kim blew imaginary bubbles in the air.

Kim's mind wandered to Norma. Oh, what she would give to be a fly on the wall right now. She could only imagine what she would think, once she found out. Hah! There she was, Mrs. Jim Whaley, now. She eyed her twenty-four karat diamond ring and smiled proudly.

She had done well. She had taken Norma's husband, 30% of her company would be partially hers (though she thought the judge quite unfair. Why not honor the document?) After all, she was now his wife. Norma had to acknowledge that.

Kim wanted much more, so much more. She wanted to destroy Norma Richmond. She wanted to see her suffer. She wanted her to beg her for mercy. Kim reflected back to what Norma had said in the courtroom.

"It isn't over, Kim," Norma had yelled in front of the entire courtroom.

"How right you are, Norma dear. Time to play ...." Kim said aloud to the breezy afternoon air.

"Kim ...," Jim was beginning to awake. His hand reached out to find that his wife was not there at his side. He became restless, tossing around in bed. Kim crawled back in bed and into his arms. Satisfied, he made himself comfortable and went back to sleep.

"Yes, it's only the beginning," Kim whispered softly to herself before closing her eyes to get a little more sleep.

Norma and Jonathon sat in Taix on Sunset Boulevard, a quaint French restaurant in the center of town. Norma sighed deep before sipping on her wine.

"Thank you, Jon. I really needed this," Norma said, putting down her wine glass.

"What, the wine?" Jon said, making Norma laugh. Her smile could light up any room. He wanted to keep her laughing.

"No, you just need to relax more. I know that this divorce thing has got you really tensed up, but that part of your life is over. I refuse to allow you to stress over Jim Whaley in my presence. He's just not worth it!" Jon was grateful that the food was arriving. He was starving, and could not have imagined better company with which to share his meal. Norma was truly a delight.

"Since you are on the subject again, where is that jerk? I fully expected he and Kim to come to my office and gloat in my face by now?" Norma tasted her dish and nodded with satisfaction.

Jon stopped chewing and wiped his brow.

Norma looked puzzled at Jon's expression, "What? ... why are you looking at me like that? What is it, Jon?"

"I noticed that you had not mentioned it ... I assumed it was why you had so much extra tension, I ..." Jon did not want to be the one to deliver another blow. She did not deserve that, but she had to know the truth.

"Jon, what is it?" Norma edged him on. She just would not let it go.

"Norma, it's in all the trash magazines by now," Jon hesitated, holding his fork, and bobbing it back and forth.

"Jon, please ... just tell me what could it possibly be?" Norma said, her curiosity outweighing any sense of anger or hurt by this point. After all, how could it be all that bad?

"Okay ... Jim and Kimberley flew to Vegas to be married this weekend. They're probably married by now." Norma dropped her glass, spilling the wine she was about to drink. It *was bad,* very bad.

The waitress scurried over to clean the mess. Norma swallowed hard, as she felt a sharp pain shoot from her heart to her stomach. I mean, he could not even wait one week before he married her. She had loved him so much at one time. He had never loved her at all.

Jon reached for her hand. "Are you okay?" Jon was concerned that she might faint by the look on her face. Norma pulled her hand away.

"Yes, I'm fine," Norma lied, and made an effort at enjoying the rest of their meal.

"Well, there's one more thing before ..."

"What is it?" Norma said regretfully. She might as well get it all out in the open now.

"The contract you signed ... it included one small clause ... "

Jon paused again, making Norma react in anger, "Dammit Jon! Tell me now!" Jon appeared a little shocked at her tone with him. It was understandable, considering what she was going through.

"Oh, I'm sorry Jon," Norma realized that her tone had been rather harsh with him.

Jon hesitated but finally continued, "The clause states that should Kimberley marry Jim, she would then be entitled to access her husband's 30% ... and must be given a company title ... deemed by you. Norma ... the woman covered her bases here. What can I say?" Norma's eyes seemed to roll to the back of her head.

Jon was not sure what else to say. He had been a bearer of bad news for the day. Norma looked shattered.

"I ... I'm just speechless ... I feel like the whole world is on my shoulders," Norma fought back the tears.

"I'm here for you, you know that right? Not just as your

lawyer, but as a friend," Jon now caressed her soft diminutive hand. It was the only form of physical touch she had allowed all afternoon, without withdrawing. Norma nodded in gratitude for his kindness. She knew that he was being sincere.

Norma remained uncomfortably silent for the rest of lunch. They were both glad when the check finally came, and it was time to exit the restaurant.

They walked out of the restaurant in a somber mood. Jon accompanied Norma to her car door.

"Look. I'm sorry about lunch. You were so nice, and I ..." Norma began.

"This is a hard time for you. Divorce is hard, for anyone. I have only known you for these two years, and you have shown more integrity and honesty than most of my colleagues."

Norma chuckled a little, "Thanks, I think..."

"See, there goes that smile, again. Just remember, I'm your friend. All you need do is pick up the phone," Jon reached out his arms to Norma. She pulled gently away. Jon wanted so badly to embrace her. He resisted. She had been rejecting most of his attempts to touch her all afternoon. He knew that it was because of everything that was going on, but he could not help wondering if she found him even the least bit attractive.

Clouds were gathering in the sky, and beginning to look as dark as Norma's heart felt now. Norma began to unlock her car door, "Looks like rain, I guess we made lunch just in time."

"Hey, remember, call me if you need to talk." Jon walked towards his Mercedes, and pulled out his keys.

"I will," Norma knew that she would not call. Instead, she would go home and sulk, trying to chase away the rain in her own heart.

Chapter
<u>10</u>

Starting Over

Charles Brookton sat at his office making last minute phone calls, when the new Mr. and Mrs. Jim Whaley pranced into his New York office, arm and arm. Jonathon Newman soon followed.

Brookton began with the formal introductions, "I *would* like to say that I'm glad to see you Jim, but I'm not. I would like to introduce the both of you to ..."

"Jonathon Newman, I'm afraid we have already met," Jim said, pulling out a chair for Kimberley to sit down.

Kim was draped from head to toe with pink cashmere and shoes to match. Even Brookton had to admit to himself that she was quite stunning.

"So, we finally meet, Mrs. Whaley," Brookton began as Kim extended her pink-gloved hand to him.

"Charmed," Brookton obliged her by kissing her gloved hand.

"I would like to get the proceedings under way if you don't mind?" Jonathon said, interrupting their greetings.

"Will Norma be present for this meeting?" Kim inquired. All three gentleman turned to glare at her.

"No, I will be representing Ms. Richmond today ... uh ... Mrs. Whaley," Jon said, opening his briefcase. Jon was un-impressed by her beauty. He liked her even less than Jim. Jon continued, "Concerning Ecstacy Enterprises profit shares and corporation for the New York office. Norma Richmond has decided that the title of chief executive officer will be retained by Charles Brookton. Jim Whaley will assume position as assistant chief director, answering directly to Charles Brookton and to Norma Richmond. As for Kim Whaley ..." Kim arched her eyebrow in anticipation.

Jon continued, "Kim Whaley will assume the position as chief fashion coordinator. Your offices will ..."

"Fashion coordinator?" Kim yelled out inappropriately. Jim squeezed her hand to calm her. Kim could not contain herself, the audacity of Norma's demotion was just too much. She would not keep silent. She had worked too hard, and waited too long for this moment.

"Can you please wait until I am finished to make comments?" Jon paused, making direct eye contact with Kim, and then continuing.

"The 30% of the shares will be divided ..."

"No! you tell me why she wants me to be a damn fashion coordinator? I want some respect. I am Mrs. ..."

"Please, Mrs. Whaley, if you can not keep quiet for these proceedings you will have to leave," Brookton looked to Jim to quiet his wife. Kim kept interrupting every time that Jon began, until Jim eventually had to escort Kim out of the room. Jim practically pushed her out of the room and into the hall for a confrontation.

"Kim, what the hell is your problem?" Jim whispered, grabbing on to his wife's arm.

Kim wiggled her arm away harshly, "First the judge cuts back the 50% I worked so hard to get us, then the alimony, and now she wants to make me a damn fashion coordinator? I was her best model. She will not just ... just throw me a cookie, and expect me to run and fetch," Kim was not concerned about cordial behavior at this point. Staff members were beginning to suspect a problem. Jim tried to smile at all who passed by, as Kim raged on.

"Baby, we have won for now. We have got 30% of the profits to a company worth millions of dollars, and positions. These positions don't mean anything. They are just protocol," Jim rubbed her back now, smiling at curious onlookers. What more did this woman want? He knew that she had ambition, but this was too much.

By this time, Jon and Brookton were on their way out. Jim placed himself in the middle of Jon and Charles.

"Hey, what about the rest of the meeting? We were coming back ... we ..."

"Look, Jim, Mr. Whaley ... or whatever ... I have a business to run. I was here to represent my client. I feel that we offered the two of *you* a more than fair deal. You can review it in the copy of the written contract which I have provided for Mr. Brookton here. Oh ... and off the record. You had both better watch your back. One wrong move, and the deal's off. We are all watching both of you," Jon treaded away, leaving Jim and Kimberley speechless in his tracks.

"Why don't I show you two around," Brookton stood there grinning.

Jim and Kimberley looked at each other and sighed. There was the in-house watchdog smiling in their faces.

"Why don't you do that." Kim put on her cool charm, and took Brookton by the arm. Jim followed behind them like a faithful puppy dog.

Norma sat exploding with laughter, as Jon recanted the meeting piece by piece to her later that afternoon. The fireplace blazed, as they enjoyed a glass of Chablis at Norma's home. Jon had called her from his cell phone on the way from the airport. Instead of going home to his empty bachelor condominium, he decided to go over the sordid details with his favorite client.

It had been eight months since the divorce, and much time had been spent preparing that offer which so displeased Kim.

"For the life of me, I can not fathom what that woman wants. I mean, she has my hus ... She has Jim. She has 30% of the profits of one of my companies, much to my chagrin. I even set her up with a title and position which she in *no* way deserves. What does she care *what* it is!" Norma complained.

Jon sat back and eyed Norma with a warm expression. He admired this woman more as each day passed. They had been forced to spend a lot of time together, and now he wanted to take it to another level. Norma noticed the far away look in his eyes.

"Jon?" Norma said, as Jon shook himself back into reality.

"Yes, I keep asking myself the same question ... uh Norma?"

Jon was ready to express the way he felt. The warmth of the fireplace seemed to glisten off of his handsome brown face.

"Yes?" Norma was curious to know why he had this serious expression.

"Uh ... uh nothing, I just guess it's late and I had better head out," Jon was a little disappointed in himself. The timing had to be perfect.

"Yeah, I guess it is late," Norma sat up attentively. Jon sure looked handsome in his new gray suit. She had so much respect for him. To think, in all the months they had been working together, he had never tried to hit on her once. She wondered now if he was at all attracted to her. She knew that an attractive man such as he had many female admirers.

Jon arose from his seat, and put his hand in his pocket. Norma looked at his half-empty wine glass.

"Are you going to be okay driving home?" Norma asked, concerned for someone she now considered her good friend.

"Oh, yeah, haven't touched it for over an hour," Jon gazed in her beautiful brown eyes. He could melt in those brown eyes. He wanted to grab her, and tell her how beautiful she was, and how much he wanted her.

"Listen, I will keep you abreast of things. I will call Jim's lawyer so that we can solidify this agreement. Call you tomorrow." Norma walked Jon to the door.

"Oh, Jon, I hope it's okay, not unprofessional to say. I really uh ... I really enjoyed this evening. You went out of your way to come over, and tell me how things went." Norma pressed her toes in the bottom of her shoes, waiting anxiously for his response.

"Yes well, it's always a pleasure Norma," Jon backed away, almost slipping off the second marble step. Now, he really felt stupid.

"Hey, watch that step, now. Have a safe drive home," Norma sighed. That was not the response she had been looking for. Oh well.

Norma watched as Jon got into his car and drove away. She then resigned to take a nice, hot, bubble bath, and prepare for the next work day.

"Now hear me ladies. Every morning I want you to report to my office, and we will go over the schedule for the day's work. Things are going to be much different around this place," Kim said to a small gathering of Ecstacy's new recruits. The models exchanged puzzled looks. Charles Brookton entered to find out what the commotion was all about.

"Uh, Kim, what are you doing? There is no scheduled meeting for today," Brookton said, not quite sure how he was going to handle the habits of this pesky woman.

"Well, I want to change a few things around here. My husband and I have discussed it, and ..." Kim began.

"Listen Mrs. Whaley ... no changes can be made in any portion of Ecstacy Enterprises unless it is approved by the CEO, and that is still Ms. Norma Richmond, the last time that I checked. Any minor concerns, you bring it to me, you understand?" Brookton said calmly, but with authority.

110

"Yes, well um ..." Kim began.

Brookton quickly eyed his watch and kept talking, "Now you and I both know that those phony positions are in name only, so why don't you just go somewhere and do what you do best ..."

Kim peered at him with hateful eyes and pouched lip, "Oh, and what's that?" Kim enfolded her arms, anxiously awaiting his response.

"Lay flat on your back and let the good times roll," Brookton said, shaking his head at her as she stormed away.

Kim entered the restroom breathless, with a tear stricken face. He had no right to speak to her that way. She deserved respect. She was a wife now, and like it or not, she was an executive in this company. Norma would not throw her two pennies and expect her to walk away. No, this was a war. She would win, one battle at a time. She just needed an entirely new game plan.

Chapter
<u>11</u>

Little Surprises

"Honey, what's going on in the news? You have hardly said a word this evening?" Jim said to his wife. They enjoyed a dinner of stuffed chicken breasts, red potatoes, and lightly steamed asparagus at their New York penthouse. Kim picked at her food, and thumbed through the newspaper. Her mind meandered to and fro.

"What honey? I ... I wasn't paying attention, I ..."

"Kim, you have been acting strange lately. Have you been feeling okay?" Jim was relieved that she was no longer distracted.

"No ... it's just that no one will listen to what I have to say. The models hate me, and ..."

"Baby, is that what this is about? Why is that so important? We are making profits in our sleep. All we have to do is show up for the meetings. You don't think that Norma *really* expects you to *do* anything, do you? No, she wants nothing to do with either one of us. Baby, just be happy. You have the title. Look, you are still getting a few print jobs. Not to mention your husband absolutely adores you," Jim reached over to plant a wet kiss on her cheek.

For once in his life, Jim was perfectly content. As far as he was concerned he now had everything that he wanted—money, a sexy wife, and a title. Women! They were never satisfied.

Kim looked at her husband as though she were seeing him for the first time. He was like a kid in a candy store. He had disappointed her so. How dare he sit there content, when she was perfectly miserable.

Charles Brookton and the other models were being so hateful towards her. She had no time to get her bearing before the next attack. Jim was never there enough to see what was going on, and it seemed as if he cared about it even less. What had happened to the Jim she had married—the Jim driven by his anger and hate just as she was? She had thought their hatred of Norma was mutual. Now, he was just obeying her orders just as everyone else. He was turning into a real sap, and she hated that even more.

Kim threw down her plate, much like a spoiled child. Kim ran towards their bedroom, as Jim quickly followed to console her. She was sick of trying to explain it to him. Her emotions seemed to be getting the best of her lately.

"Kim baby, what is it?" Jim scurried to his wife's side—as she knelt down beside the bathroom door and wept.

"Jim, I just want some respect. I just want more ..." Kim whimpered.

Jim knelt down beside his sulking wife, cuddling her to him closely. He smoothed his large hand over her smooth skin, inhaling the soft scents of her hair.

Except for these occasional outbursts, Kim was the perfect woman for him. She matched his every need, in and out of bed. He could not understand what made her like this. She went to a dark place sometimes, and she never allowed him in. What was eating at her? What made her so angry? He wanted so much to give her everything that she wanted and needed, if she would only allow it.

"Look, I will talk to Charles Brookton for you. Maybe there is something that he could say or do ...," Jim began.

"No, he will only tell Norma ... don't," Kim recalled his cruel words to her. Everyone at Ecstacy sees her as a joke. She was the slut that stole the boss' husband. She would prove them all wrong.

Jim sat there puzzled at his wife's obvious distress. He so desperately wanted to help her, "Well, what can I ..."

"Shhh," Kim sensuously put her finger on his mouth. Jim obliged her, tasting her finger, and then kissing her hand softly. Whatever the case, at least their sex life was still in tact.

Kim hungrily kissed her husband, thrusting her tongue into his mouth. Jim responded by tightly grasping her wrists. They leaned against one another, kissing passionately as they attempted to stand.

Jim peeled away pieces of Kim's clothing, as she unbuttoned his shirt. It was not long before Jim picked her up, and carried her off to bed.

The evening sky was beginning to dress the newly sunset sky, when Jon walked Norma to her front door. They had spent a wonderful afternoon sharing a light picnic lunch at Griffith Park.

Jon had finally worked up the nerve to ask her out, after all of the time they had spent together. He had also suggested that she find another attorney, realizing his growing interest in her. Norma had surprised him when she smiled and said yes to both propositions. Jon was relieved. She had been a great client, but she would be an even better love interest.

Jon had thrown away his black book, and ended his two-year affair with his secretary. He wanted to make a clean break from everyone and everything. He felt that he and Norma deserved that chance.

Poor Sandra. She had fully expected him to become serious about the relationship, and marry her. He had never misled her, but was straightforward from the beginning. Nevertheless, she had not handled things well. He was almost afraid it would become one of those fatal attractions. She had called his home and cursed him several times and had even shown up there unannounced. As a result, he had no choice but to relieve her of her duties, which only fanned the fire more. She accused him of sleeping with the new secretary, before there *was a* new secretary. Looking at Norma now, with the light wind blowing through her hair and glowing eyes, it all seemed worth it now. He was free to love her.

Norma looked beautiful with highlights of red in her lustrous black hair. The long sun dress that she was wearing tailored the sensuous curves of her slender body. He wanted her so badly. He wanted to tell her and show how much he cared for her. He thought that he might even be falling in love with her. He just had no idea how to express his true feelings. He was not sure of what her reaction would be.

"I had such a good time, Jon. It's been such a wonderful afternoon, " Norma said, as Jon edged closer to her.

"Yeah, so did I ...," Jon managed. They both sat there fidgeting under her porch light, trying to ponder what to say next.

"You know I ..." they both began in unison.

"Ladies first," Jon opened his palm towards her.

"I was going to say that ... um ... it was such a wonderful day, I almost hate to see it end."

"Then, why let it end?" Jon now pulled her closer, no longer able to resist the urge to kiss her. Why not jump in with both feet running? Jon's breathing became sporadic and hard.

His lips gently touched the tip of her nose, while his hands closed in tighter around her waist. Norma smiled, welcoming this friendly kiss, as Jon's lips finally found their way to her mouth. He enticed her with his warm, wet kisses, beginning small, and growing longer and more involved.

"Jon, no ... no it's just too soon," Norma gently pushed him away. Norma wanted him too, but not like this, not now. She was still healing on the inside. Jim had hurt her so bad, and Jon deserved her whole heart.

"Oh, I am ... I'm sorry ... I should go ... I should ..." Jon was quite embarrassed at his erection in clear view. Norma's expression revealed that she too was aware of his excitement.

He nervously backed away, and practically ran towards his car.

Norma was embarrassed, not quite sure what to say either. Norma stood there speechless. This beautiful, usually composed man stood in the dark, fumbling around for his key. He finally managed to open his car door.

"I'll call you tomorrow ... I," he mumbled, quickly planting himself behind the wheel, and pulling out of her driveway.

Norma blushed a little, and then finally let go of a small giggle. It was nice to know that someone thought that she was still an attractive woman. Jim had made her feel like a "dirty old woman". I guess she was not out of the game after all.

Norma opened the door to her home anxious, not knowing how she would possibly get to sleep that night. She was too ready for the next day of life's new adventures.

Kim awoke from her blissful sleep with a horrible stomachache. She rushed to the toilet, and made it just in time to regurgitate. Her coughing awoke Jim.

Jim rushed over to his wife to see her bent over into the toilet.

"Honey, you are sicker than I thought. Why don't we get you to the hospital right away," Jim began, concerned for the woman he loved. Maybe all of this stress was making her sick.

"I'm just a little sick, it was probably something I ate," Kim threw a dismissive wave. Jim prepared to drive to the hospital despite her protests.

"Honey, I think you should really get some counseling or something. All of this stress is really getting to you."

Kim rolled her eyes at her husband. Now he was beginning to sound like a father. Whatever happened to the old Jim?

Jim had already gathered her coat and all of his things to take her to the hospital.

"Jim, I'm telling you, it's just ..."

"Look, I don't want to hear anymore. You are going and that's it!" Jim insisted, now forcing her arm inside a coat he had grabbed from the closet.

"Okay, daddy, but can I at least put on some clothes. You wouldn't want me to go in my nightie?" Kim whined in a small child-like voice.

Jim nodded as Kim walked back towards her bedroom closet.

"Ta ole' Sap," Kim muttered aloud.

"What was that?" Jim was unable to make out what she said.

"Oh, nothing honey," Kim reluctantly grabbed a jumpsuit from the closet and slipped it on. Jim would not relent.

Kim emerged from the bedroom dressed and waving a peace sign. Jim helped her put on her coat, and they headed for the door.

Two hours later ...

Kim stared into the face of her doctor in obvious disbelief, "Pregnant? You have got to be kidding?" This was not in *her* plan. She had been on the pill. Was this some kind of a joke?

"Yes, Mrs. Whaley, about three weeks, and I suggest you get more rest, and stop being so stressed out about work. Your husband expressed concern to me," the Doctor began. Jim let go of a proud yell.

"Oh, yes!" Jim proudly lifted his wife in the air spinning her around, "I knew it! This is the best news, baby. I couldn't be happier." This also explained her mood swings and crying spells, poor thing.

"Jim, I, I ...." Kim muttered weakly.

"Don't talk now, sweetheart. We are going home. I am gonna take such good care of you, baby. It's really gonna be all right," he helped her stand to her feet. He felt as if he would explode with joy. He would be the best father, better than his father had ever been for him.

Jim reflected briefly on his father's habit of beating him to a pulp for anything and everything. He would be a much different father. He would listen to his son, and show him love. He looked lovingly into his wife's eyes, the mother-to-be. He would give her all of the support that she needed. They would not yell, argue and fist fight in front of their child. They would not drink and get high in front of their children, the way his parents had done. This child would have a much better life than he. Jim would see to that.

An elated Jim practically skipped out of the hospital, and meticulously helped his wife from the parking lot to their car. He was too helpful, as far as Kim was concerned. He wanted her barefoot and pregnant, totally dependent on him.

Kim pouted, as he adjusted her seat in a reclining position so that she could relax. Jim kissed her gently on her lips, before making his way to the driver's seat. A wave of nausea swept over Kim again, so she opened the car door just in case she had to release.

Jim now shut his own door. Visions of fatherhood, and the family times ahead flashed through his head. Now, he would have the chance to have his own family. He had never loved Kim more than he did at this moment. Now their love would be forever held in time through a child, their child. Jim whisked his fingers through his wife's hair.

"Just rest baby. Everything will work out fine," Jim whispered softly.

Kim closed her eyes and pretended to sleep. She was already plotting in her head ways to get out of this mess. This was all Norma's fault. If she had not been so busy worrying about her and that damn company, she would never have been so careless. She would have to make her pay.

Jim sighed in complete satisfaction and euphoria. He focused his eyes on the dark road ahead, ensuring his family a safe journey home.

* * *

Two weeks later ...

Norma sat in her Los Angeles office on an important business call, when her office door flew open. Kim intruded, the secretary racing at her heels. Norma explained to her client that she would have to call back later.

"I am sorry Ms. Richmond, I just could not stop her, I ..." Casey began.

"It's okay Casey, just alert security," Norma spoke calmly, as Casey scurried towards the door.

Norma maintained her monotone voice, " Kim, what in the hell do you want?" Norma was no longer willing to be upset or moved by this woman's actions.

Kim glared at Norma, her eyes filled with an obsessive hatred. Norma had not seen Kim since she had learned of her pregnancy. Kim had begged Jim to let her take his place at a Los Angeles meeting, just so she could face Norma. He had ordered her to steer clear of Norma while on her visit.

Norma was rather surprised at Kim's appearance. Usually a stunning creature, her hair was rather disheveled, and her clothes too tight fitting. Norma noticed her weight gain, her pregnancy just now beginning to show. New York did not agree with her.

"You will be delighted to know that Jim has agreed to let me act in his place as assistant chief for operations in New York," Kim said, never letting go of her vicious stare. Jim had agreed to no such thing. In fact, it took all of her coaxing just to let her take his place at the meeting, given her "fragile" condition. She just could not resist the urge to stop by and torture her mortal enemy, while in town. Besides, Kim was enjoying the reaction she was getting from Norma.

"You flew all the way to Los Angeles to tell me that my *stupid* ex-husband is letting you take his position. I'm surprised.

He worked so hard for it. He should probably get an Oscar for his award winning performances." Norma twisted her mouth a little to make her disgust more apparent.

"No, I flew *all* the way to Los Angeles to tell you that Jim and I are expecting a baby," Kim recanted, with a devilish grinning. Norma's eyes dropped.

For a moment, there was complete silence in the room. Norma was stunned by the news. She finally retorted, "Frankly my dear, I really don't give a damn."

Norma lied, she did care. That hurt. She had wanted a baby, Jim's baby. She had wanted to fill that house with little children. Little voices echoed in her head. Why did this conniving little witch deserve that chance she never had? Kim could see it all over her face.

Kim needled her more, "I'm giving him something you never could." Norma's insides were set aflame, as two security guards finally arrived to collect Kim.

"Ma'am, would you please come with us?" one guard said, the other calmly waiting at the door.

Kim gave Norma one more hateful look, before prancing towards the guards. She was satisfied with Norma's obvious distress. Norma watched, as the guard escorted Kim out, and finally shut the door.

Norma stared at the door for several moments, replaying the recent events in her mind. In a way, she felt sorry for the woman. It must be tiring to carry around so much hate. She could not understand what she possessed that the woman so desperately wanted. She had Jim. She even had a share in a 30% profit with one of her companies, and a phony title. What more could she possibly give her? Who did she think she was to come in her office and demand anything of her? Kim needed serious help. She was obviously using her as a pawn to vent out some sick, displaced anger. But why was she on a mission to make a personal enemy of her? If anyone should have wanted revenge, it should have been Norma. The woman must be suffering from some sort of strange emotional disorder. She would have no choice but to mention it to Jim. The judge had ordered her to sign away a piece of her company, but she would not be harassed by that nit wit! Norma shook her head, and then took a few deep calming breaths. The phone rang, startling her a bit.

"Shows over," Norma announced to the spectators that had gathered at her door. She pressed her lips into the receiver, "Hello."

"Hello ... uh Norma," a sexy low voice mumbled at the other end.

"Oh, Jon ... Hi," Norma beamed with elation. She had not spoken to him since their little incident.

"You wouldn't believe who just stepped out of my office ..." Norma began.

"Who?" Jon said, relieved that she had no hang ups about the other night.

"Our favorite brunette," Norma chuckled. It was their little joke about Kim. Jon's laughter on the other end made her smile.

"Kim, what was she doing there? Listen, why don't you tell me over dinner, assuming that you ever want to see me again after the other night?" he said, clearing his throat.

"Oh, what are you talking about? Listen, I will meet you only if you let me treat this time," Norma was anxious to put his fears at bay. He was so polite, and such a gentleman. He was always concerned about her feelings, and she admired that.

"Okay, I can even stop by and pick you up, if you'd like?" Jon was relieved that she did not feel disrespected in any way. He had not wanted to damage their friendship or budding relationship. After all, that black book was now gone—he was playing for keeps.

"I would like," Norma was so happy that he had decided to call. She had wanted to give him time to get over any embarrassment.

"See you at 7:30," Jon cooed soft and sensually.

"Seven-thirty then," Norma grinned to herself like a teenager. Despite Kim's imprudent behavior, her evening would not be ruined after all.

Chapter
<u>12</u>

Thoughts of Malice

"Mrs. Whaley, this is something that I hate to do, especially without your husband's consent," Dr. Mallords explained carefully. Kim stretched and pulled her knuckles apathetically.

It had only been two weeks since returning from what Jim had labeled the "Norma incident". Jim had the nerve to suggest that she seek counseling for her "Norma obsession". Now, Kim sat staring into the eyes of this doctor, asking him to take away their child.

Jim had been so happy about this whole pregnancy thing, but it was really starting to slow her down. She was sick all of the time, and hardly making it to work. Her mood swings were getting worse, and she was getting way too fat. She knew what she had to do. Jim would never even have to know.

"Just do it. I'll pay you ... whatever you want," Kim said without reservation. She could not be hindered by a baby right now. There was no other choice. She never pictured herself as the June Cleaver type, anyway.

"Would you like to see a counselor, maybe? We can set it up, and your regular doctor can ..." Dr. Mallords began, searching for any sense of conscious or hesitation from her.

"No. Look, this is why I came here. So, if you won't do it, I can get someone else who will! I can take my money elsewhere!" Kim raged.

He saw that she would not relent, and finally nodded at the nurse to prepare for the procedure.

Kim was directed to a small room, and asked to disrobe. Soon, the nurse appeared, and instructed her to lie back. The doctor appeared shortly after, instructing her to placed her feet in the stirrups. Kim inflated her cheeks and closed her eyes, as the doctor pressed the needle into her skin.

It was not long before the drug took its affect. Kim's mind drifted back to memories of her mother and childhood. She could remember her mother's old rocking chair swinging back and forth, making creaking sounds with the passing wind. It was as if she were a little child of eight again, there in the back yard on her favorite swing. She was there again, under her mother's watchful eye.

Her mother's sweet, round face haunted her, the memories pouring in like a flood. She could hear her mother's voice calling in the distance to come in for supper.

"Kimmie, Kimmie," momma would call. She would run pass the swing to the back door, looking for mommy. Mommy would stand there with open arms waiting to hold her, and protect her from the world.

"Mommy ... mommy," Kim muttered aloud, the anesthesia wearing down, as the procedure came to its end. She slowly began coming back into consciousness, her memory shifting forward and faster now. It shifted to her mother's funeral, those years of being an unwanted orphan, after her mother's death. Then, there were those years of physical abuse from several foster parents. The rape at fifteen replayed in her mind like a recurring nightmare, so vivid, so horrible, so mind shattering.

Kim's eyes fluttered, as she recalled the night that changed her life forever. There she was in that dark dreary room again, staring at the dull, grayish carpet. She listened for his footsteps, afraid, helpless, hopeless. She had tried to climb out of the window, but he had opened the door and dragged her by her feet with his long, muscular arms. He shook her hard, slapping her so that the blood flowed freely from her aching mouth.

He had come before, but this time was different. Even now, she could smell his musky scent, taste the alcohol on his breath. His red, watery eyes told her that something else was on his mind.

Kim kicked and scratched at him, as he tore her white blouse and forced her skirt above her waist. She had managed a few screams before he pressed his sweaty hand hard against her mouth to silence her. She felt so small and helpless, as he pressed his large, overbearing body on her frail frame. She was hardly able to breathe, his weight crushing her.

Kim suddenly felt a sharp pain, pressing in between her thighs. Somehow he was inside of her, hurting her, killing her. It sent shocks through her, the pain almost unbearable. She thought that she would die.

He had taken her body, used and discarded her like a dirty dish rag. With him, went what little was left of her youth, innocence, and sense of self worth. He had made her feel so dirty inside that she would bathe five times a day to get the smell out of her skin, and off of her soul.

She had tried to tell counselors, friends, even the man's wife. No one had believed the word of a troubled kid, just like he had said. It only made things worse.

She had been passed around like a frisbie, from household to household. She had fought off male foster caretakers, until finally deciding to run away.

There had been no sign of a father. Momma had always promised that he would come for them, one day. But she had died, and Daddy had never come, never.

No one had loved her. No one had wanted her. No one except her mother, and she was gone now. Kim blinked the flow of tears away, and fought the memories, too painful to remember now. It sometimes resurfaced when Jim touched her a certain way. She would automatically pull away. She buried those memories deep again, where no one would ever find them.

Kim was a bit groggy coming out of it, but fully conscious an hour later. As the lights came into full focus, the nurse appeared and helped her put on her clothes. Dr. Mallords appeared several moments later, with a long list of do's and don'ts, after the ordeal her body had just endured.

Kim waited a few moments to gather her strength, but then began to gather her things. The doctor continued speaking. Kim helped herself down, and headed for the door. The doctor began speaking faster, as the nurse pleaded with her to rest for a while, "Please ma'am your body is in shock. You will not want to drive now!" Kim ignored her, turning the doorknob.

"Mrs. Whaley, would you like me to call you to give you these instructions? Would you like someone to come and pick...?" Dr. Mallords began, as Kim opened the door to exit, "But Mrs. Whaley ... you can't just ... walk out ..." he said, but Kim had already slammed the door behind her.

"What an awful woman. I feel sorry for the poor bastard that married her," Dr. Mallords commented to his nurse, who only shrugged her shoulders and went about her way cleaning up the surrounding area.

Kim opened her front door to find an enraged and worried Jim. It had taken much longer than she had anticipated, and Jim was a raving lunatic by this late hour. She had not seen him since that morning. Kim closed the door behind her, blinking her blurry eyes and touching her feverish head.

"Kim, where in the hell have you been? I have been so worried. In *your* condition, you should really be lying down," Jim sounded much like a concerned father.

Kim looked at him, and sighed. Even *she* did not have the heart to tell him that she had killed their baby, a baby that he had wanted. He would be crushed. Kim took his advice, and collapsed in their bed.

She awoke several hours later to a horrible pain in her stomach. She screamed out in pain, as she noticed the fresh blood on her sheets. She ran to the bathroom leaving a trail of blood behind her.

"Jim!" Kim managed to cry out. Jim awoke to find his wife curled up in pain on the floor, tears streaming down her face.

"Oh Jim, I don't know what's happening. There is something I need to tell you about the baby ... I ..." Kim began as pain silenced her. She screamed out in pain, grasping her stomach with one hand. She reached out to her husband with the other hand.

"Shhhh ... baby ... everything is gonna be fine. I love you so much. I promise I'll take care of you," Jim wrapped a blanket around her, gathered her coat, and carried her downstairs to their car.

Later that night ...

"Mrs. Whaley," Dr. Mallords whispered softly, as Kim blinked her eyes trying to adjust to the lights.

"What? Where am I ? How long have I been out ...?" Kim muttered, turning to see Jim leaning against the transparent hospital door.

Kim suddenly turned to the doctor, "You didn't tell Jim about the ..."

"No, he assumes that you had a miscarriage. Abortion can be hard on any woman's body. I was instructing you to be much more cautious this afternoon when you ..." the doctor began.

"Thanks, that will be enough," Kim interrupted. She certainly did not feel like a lecture right now. Jim stumbled in the room looking dejected. It was obvious that he had high hopes for this baby.

"Kim, baby it's gonna be all right. We can try again." Tears welled in Jim's hazel eyes, making them red and swollen-like.

"Is he for real?" Kim thought to herself. Jim stood there trying to comfort her. Boy, was he turning into an old sappy man, old and sentimental. There was no sign of the co-conspirator who had once plotted with her to take Norma down. He *had* everything *he* wanted. He was perfectly satisfied, and perfectly disgusting to Kim.

"Oh baby, I thought I was gonna lose you. You just took on too much stress. You just can't do that to yourself. Sweetheart, say, why don't we get out of here for a couple of days, take a vacation. We can go anywhere you want," Jim kissed her hand as she lay there in the hospital bed, callous and indifferent.

Nurse Rita Abney entered the room, rescuing her from this sickening melodrama, "Mr. Whaley, I am sorry, but I am going to have to ask you to leave now. Visiting hours are over. Your wife must rest to regain her strength."

Nurse Rita admired Jim's affection towards his wife. He was not the horrible guy that the tabloids had portrayed. It was obvious how much he loved this woman.

"Yes, I will be right outside if you need me. I will be here first thing when you wake up," Jim said, reluctantly backing away.

"Goodbye, Mr. Whaley," the nurse said, smiling and waving to him. Jim blew Kim one final kiss before leaving. Kim wanted to throw up. She turned her head towards her pillow.

"Whoosh," Kim let out in relief, once she knew that he was gone. The nurse shook her head a little. You would think she would be happy that her husband loved her that much. I guess she *was* as bad as the tabloids had said.

The nurse had recognized her the minute she had been admitted. She had heard from her nurse friend about the "secret" abortion.

"Here, Mrs. Whaley, brought something to help you get to sleep," Nurse Rita handed her two white pills and a small cup of water. Kim gulped down the pills and took a sip of water.

"Thanks ... uh Rita," Kim noted her white name tag. She might as well get on her good side. Rita smiled a bit, handing her a couple of magazines to read, since she did not seem interested in the television.

"Nice, guy, your hubby," Rita could not help but to mention it.

"Yeah, he's all right," Kim said nonchalantly but offered nothing more.

The nurse quickly finished her round and exited. Kim sat there bored, fiddling through some of the magazines. She noticed that many of the models were from Ecstacy. She browsed through another. Lo and behold, there was a story about Norma Richmond inside—on her rise to success.

Kim maliciously thrust the magazine across the room with all of her might. God, how she despised that woman! Why should Norma have everything, and she not have a piece of it all?

She thought about their last meeting, and how upset Norma seemed at the idea of her having Jim's baby. She had never known that the old bat even had a maternal desire in her ambitious brain. Now that the baby was gone, Norma would probably be happy about it. Norma would never admit it to herself, being such the self-righteous martyr, always the victim.

Flipping through the magazines gave Kim a genius idea. Without the models, Ecstacy would crumble. And without Ecstacy, Norma would be nothing. That was it! She had to find a way to turn Norma's models against her, once and for all. But how could she do that? Norma's reputation was practically immaculate.

Once Norma was destroyed, maybe she could get the backing to create her own company. Maybe she would call it Whaley ... no ... Brandon Enterprises. But what would send Norma's girls running to her? Kim thought for a moment, placing a finger on her chin. As always, it took her no time to come up with the perfect solution. Kim yawned, the sleeping pills finally taking their effect. She closed her eyes satisfied that she had come up with the perfect plan.

Kim dashed down 5th avenue at lightning speed, intent to make it on time for her lunch appointment. It had been just six months after her so-called miscarriage.

Surprisingly enough, that whole ordeal had all worked in

her favor. Everyone was much nicer and receptive to her as a woman and as an executive. Even Norma had expressed sympathy, to Jim, to relay to her.

Jim had been wonderful, showering her with gifts, and taking her on a seven-day cruise to the Bahamas, to take her mind off of her "trauma". During that cruise, Kim convinced him to let her take a more active role in the company. Up to that point, he had let her sub for him at a few meetings, and appear at a few functions in his place. She wanted to attend all of the meetings and do the work. She wanted the authority and power to exercise her position. Then, she could move full steam ahead with her own plans. She promised him that he would not have to do anything with her in charge. Besides, she needed something to keep her busy, after such a "traumatic" experience.

Jim submitted, after seven days and nights of exquisite pleasure and intensive catering from his wife. Kim got right to work two days after her return, everyone finally willing to cooperate and give her a fresh new start.

Kim spent the first two months building a new relationship with the models. She quickly learned not to bother with the more experienced and popular models, who had much loyalty to their company and owner.

The newer, more naive clientele had as many reasons to complain and bicker as she did. All they needed was a listening ear, which Kim gladly provided. They all fussed at how ignored they were, and how the more popular models always took priority. They complained of never having a voice with the boss due to her busy lifestyle, and her obvious new love interest, her ex-attorney.

It was then that Kim would reveal her secret agenda to begin her own company, and make them the number one priority. No one knew about these secret meetings, except she and the models. They dared not say anything, in fear that she would have them immediately fired. They knew that with Kim, that was not necessarily an idle threat.

By the time Kim Whaley stepped inside a small New York café to have lunch with Fredericko Mendoza, she had at least a third of the company under her belt. That was enough to start her own company, independent of Norma Richmond. She was quite proud of herself. She had worked quite hard, and no thanks to her couch potato husband. He had really taken everything she had said to heart, doing most of his work at home. He had settled in his role as husband, and had started pressuring her about trying for another baby.

If this meeting went well, she could possibly buy Norma out of the new branch set to open in San Francisco. This potential financial investor could help her start her very own company, completely separate from the likes of Norma Richmond. This way, she could kill two birds with one stone. She could do mortal damage to her enemy's business, while securing her own future. Hell, she just wanted to see the look on Norma's face when she found out about it all. Once Norma found that her precious "girls" were baring their very souls to her, she would be crushed. It sort of made Kim feel all tingly inside.

Kim looked anxiously around. A large brown hand waved and caught her attention. Fredericko smiled, and Kim walked towards him.

Fredericko Mendoza was a tall, handsome Latino man, with broad shoulders, a muscular body, deep brown eyes, and long wavy hair, which he kept in a ponytail. He was one of the richest designers in New York City, from a entrepreneur New Jersey family. His family migrated to New Jersey from Cuba when he was just a boy. He grew up in a poor, but loving, family with three sisters and two brothers. His father and mother worked hard, but never gave up their vision of becoming internationally known fashion designers.

Caesar Eduardo Mendoza, Fredericko's father, created a line of clothing for the Latino men of his community. His mother had helped make many of the first designs in their own home. The Mendoza's eventually became very wealthy, creating designs for movie stars and the general public, their line, Innovative Design, a sweeping success for the last fifteen years.

Fredericko began his own career in his father's factories, he and his brothers working long hours. Fredericko eventually began his own line with his brother, and now here he was. He was not on the Forbes list the last time he checked, but he was getting there.

Fredericko took a sip of brandy, as Kim neared the table where he was seated. He carefully eyed her long legs, wavy hair, and beautiful light creamy toned skin. He hoped that business was not *all* she wanted to discuss this afternoon.

"Hello, Mr. Mendoza, it's a pleasure to meet you," Kim said as he stood to greet her.

"The pleasure is all mine, Senora Whaley," he said as Kim graciously extended her hand for him to kiss gently. "You are even more beautiful than any of your photographs," he licked his lips.

"Thank you, Mr. ..."

"Ah, I insist, senora, call me Fredericko," he interrupted and took out the chair for her to have a seat.

Kim ordered a glass of Chardonnay, as Fredericko inhaled her enticing floral scent.

"So, I am interested to know what this meeting is all about. You mentioned something about Ecstacy ... and ... starting a new agency over the phone?" Fredericko now finished his own brandy. He had met Jim and Kimberley at a party several months ago. Being the playboy that he was, he had slipped Kim his card—when Jim was not watching. He had never expected to hear from her after the first month passed.

"As I explained over the phone ... Fredericko ... I am considering opening up my own agency, and am in need of investors, I ..."

"Mrs. Whaley, the buzz is that you are making waves as the new assistant chief at Ecstacy here in New York. Am I to assume that your husband will resume the position, or is he to partner you in this new venture?" Fredericko said, his eyebrows raised now. He was intrigued by this stunning creature.

"Well, you see ... uh ... Fredericko, that's another issue I wanted to discuss with you," Kim edged a bit closer to him. "My husband, owns a 30% share profit of Ecstacy profit through his ex-wife, Norma Richmond. So, my position now, is but a small step in my long term goal," Kim winked and smiled coyly at Fredericko.

"Oh, I see ... and what is your long term goal?" he was fascinated by this lovely flower sitting before him.

"I was thinking," she began in a soft sexy tone, rubbing her foot against his ankle. Fredericko loosened his tie. "I was thinking ... someone with your influence and power could easily help me buy that share from Norma, and start a new company." Kim now placed her foot on his groin and placed her tongue seductively in his ear. They were interrupted by the waiter bringing Kim's wine.

"Of course, this would have to be a very, very secretive partnership in order to work. You do understand, don't you? With your money and influence, and my master deception, we could take Norma down ... I mean, buy her out," Kim now rubbed her warmth against his body.

"Why don't we go somewhere more private and discuss this?" Fredericko kissed her soft hand sensuously and grabbed his briefcase.

"Sure, why not?" Kim gathered her things. They left the café giggling and holding hands like teenagers.

A half an hour later ...

Kim and Fredericko grinned and flirted with each other, until they finally reached a nearby hotel on Seventh Avenue. They registered under the name Johnson, and rushed like love birds to their room.

Fredericko could hardly contain his aching, throbbing desire for Kim, as he shut the heavy wooden door and locked it. He placed the champagne they had stopped to buy on a nearby table, and grabbed Kim, kissing her passionately.

Fredericko abruptly stopped kissing Kim, leaving her breathless and hungry for more. He gazed directly into her eyes, whispering softly and seductively, "Aye, muy hermosa ... te quiero ... te amo senorita ...." He helped her to undo her blouse, while inhaling her soft scented skin. He slowly and meticulously planted soft, wet kisses from her chin to her shoulder blades.

Kim welcomed his anticipation, unzipping his pants, and almost tearing his shirt.

"Aye caramba! my little senorita. Slow it down. Let Don Juan show you de way," he said with a thick accent, first kissing her hand with meticulous and sensual care. He then slowly, but passionately led her towards the hotel bed, and gently placed her on it. Kim pressed her nails into the satin sheets, and grit her teeth with insatiable desire.

Fredericko whispered more words of romance and love, "Te amo ... princesa." Kim closed her eyes and pressed her head and body against the supreme coolness of silky sheets beneath her. She surrendered with uninhibited resolve to Fredericko's touch.

Kim jumped a little, as she felt something cold and wet running down her heated skin. She looked up to behold Fredericko, pouring champagne down the nape of her neck. They both laughed.

"Now, I shall dr-ink, my bonita," Fredericko spoke softly as he began licking her neck, then down to her breast, very gentle and soft, making her cry out in exquisite pleasure.

"OOOH," Kim responded. He excited her as no man had before. Kim was enthralled by the gentleness and sensuality with which he handled her body.

She then allowed him to completely undress her, as he embedded her with kisses *everywhere* from her neck to her feet. His kisses felt much like wet electricity on Kim's anxious, willing body. They both smiled in earnest delight.

He entered her only after she had reached the pinnacle of her pleasure, then completely satisfying her with every tantalizing stroke. It seemed to last forever, and they moaned in unison, reaching that final climax of passion together.

Kim drifted into a deep sleep afterwards, and awoke several hours later to find a beautiful arrangement of flowers. A note, on white lined paper, was also by the bed which read:

Thank you for an incredible afternoon. We will discuss this arrangement hopefully sooner than later. Later my senora.

Te Quiero,
Fredericko

Kim sighed, her heart full of romance, passion and school-girl frenzy. What a lover, that Fredericko! She hoped they could share many more afternoons together just like this.

Kim's bliss was soon cut short, when she caught a glimpse of her watch on the mantel. It was now 6:00 p.m. Jim would be looking for her. How would she explain?

She frantically dialed home. The answering machine picked up, and Kim struggled for the words to say. What could she tell him? The meeting held over this late? She had been in an accident? No, she would not have him worry.

Kim smiled with cool ease, as the solution came to her. She suddenly became very calm, as the beep sounded for her to leave her message, "Sweetheart, this is your darling Kimberley. Meet me at our old hotel on Seventh Avenue, suite 402. We are registered under the name Johnson. This will not be a night you will soon forget. Sorry for not calling before, I wanted to surprise you. See you soon hon," Kim tore the note, but kept the flowers. She would tell him it was all for him. She would order room service, and create the whole ambiance. She would talk to the hotel manager, and cover her tracks. Money could buy her silence. No one would peep a word of what had happened earlier. Jim would never even have to know.

Kim smiled to herself, as she reflected on her afternoon of lovemaking with Fredericko. It all seemed like a dream now. She opened the hotel window and inhaled the spring air, watching the hustle and bustle of people below her.

Fredericko had the power to make her ultimate dream come true—destroy Norma Richmond. Not to mention, he was the best lay she had had since she had married Jim. It was the first time she had been unfaithful to Jim, but she had no regrets.

Kim laughed wildly and spun around, as the busy streets of Manhattan kept turning below her, "Watch out Norma Richmond, cause I'm hot on your trail. Time to pay the toll," she laughed loudly, spinning around.

Chapter
<u>13</u>

Cinderella Brown

Fredericko Mendoza searched around LAX Airport with one suitcase in hand. The sounds of people rushing to and fro nestled in his ears. Fredericko smiled as he watched a young girl run eagerly to greet her waiting parents. He nervously eyed his watch, and tapped his foot.

Fredericko smiled with relief, as he spotted three smiling familiar faces nearby. An old wizened man came to embrace him.

"Aye, Popi," Fredericko said, as his father gripped tighter, the love oozing from his palms. The other two smiling faces came closer to greet Fredericko and his father.

"Hello, Fredericko," Norma said, Jon lagging behind.

"Buenos noches, senora Richmond," Fredericko greeted her, his father finally let go of his grip. It had been three months since they had seen one another.

"So how did it go?" Jon said, pointing to Fredericko's briefcase.

"Great! I've got it all on tape." Jon and Norma made eye contact and smiled.

"You were correct, senora Norma, she was trying to buy you out.

"I must say she was *quite* convincing ... it's a shame we could not have gotten to know one another better."

Norma had known Fredericko and his father for ten years.

He had been a teenager in high school, when Norma had made her first deal with his father. Now, they both designed many clothes for her models, and used her name and more popular models many times to enhance sells. Norma was a loyal, worthy investment and friend. Fredericko was not about to jeopardize their business and friendship relationship. Kim had been delightful, but she was not worth making an enemy of Norma Richmond.

Fredericko alerted Norma the moment that Kim had called, and took precaution to protect his investments. He placed a small tape recorder inside of his briefcase, just in case. He had no idea that Kim would so easily state her claim, and how *willing* she was to solidify the agreement.

"Hey, why don't we all go to lunch. It's been a while since we all sat down and talked," Norma continued, placing an arm around Fredericko's shoulder. After all, this could be just what the judge needed to throw that witch and her jerk of a husband out of Ecstacy for good.

Norma had been told that Kim was even trying to take some of her newer models and form her own new company. Fredericko confirmed all of that.

"So, tell me Fredericko ... how did you get her to confess?" Norma now leaned on Jon, as they all walked towards the airport exit.

"Oh, I have my ways," Fredericko smiled slyly and raising his eyebrows at all of them.

Jim stood with his mouth open, reading the subpoena that had just been delivered to their Manhattan penthouse.

"Kim!" he yelled out an almost primal call.

Kim wandered around in constant bliss, waiting for her secret lover to call. It had been a week since that memorable night, but she was not worried. She knew that he could never forget her. He was probably somewhere thinking of her as well.

"Kim, do you have any idea what this is about? Have you been making alimony payments on time?" Jim said, not having the foggiest idea as to what this could be about.

"Jim, what is it that you're going on about?" Kim snatched the subpoena. He had finally caught her attention. Kim read the subpoena, but refused to be bothered by it. She fanned her hand in dismissal.

Norma was just throwing up smoke screens now. It was all over for her now. She had finally met someone with the guts to stand up to Norma. He was not the wimp that her husband had now become. No, Fredericko had the power and money to match Norma pound for pound. She could imagine her lover standing up to Norma, and everything crumbling around her now. Even her precious Jon could not save her this time. They would make a formidable pair, much more suited than she and Jim now. She would divorce Jim as soon as ...

"Kim, dammnit! Would you stop day dreaming? What the hell are you so happy about anyway? Baby, this is very important. Apparently, we have done something to breach our contract, and I sure as hell don't know what happened. Now if you missed a few alimony payments, you better tell me, woman!" Jim insisted, picking up the phone to dial his lawyer.

Kim was certainly no help. It was as if she were Alice in Wonderland, ever since that night at the hotel. Maybe she was pregnant again, Jim thought, a smile surfacing even in his anger. He so wanted Kim to have his baby now.

Kim answered nonchalantly, running her bath water, "Well, come to think of it dear, I did miss a *few*, but I'm sure we can settle it with ole Norm, huh?" Kim danced around in a daze humming to herself.

"Kim, what the hell is wrong with you?..." Jim began ranting, but Kim could no longer hear a word he said. She was in a fantasy world where she and Fredericko were a prince and princess in a castle by a far away sea.

Kim ran the water for her bath, humming and dancing every

step of the way. What Jim said or did no longer mattered. Fredericko would come through as no man had before. He would slay the dragon, and save the princess. He would help her destroy her greatest enemy, and help save the day.

"Mrs. Kimberley Whaley, did you propose a takeover, and in fact fax Fredericko Mendoza a contractual agreement between you two parties?" Norma's lawyer demanded as everyone peered on at a dumbfounded Kim. The Los Angeles courtroom was crowded, heat settling from all of the bodies. Kim could seemingly hear every thump of the giant clock at the front of the courtroom. The judge turned her body towards Kim. Beads of sweat formed on her brow, the crowd anticipating her response.

Norma had hired a new lawyer, upon Jon's council. He was a 40 year old Robert Shapiro type from New Jersey. Marlon Steinbaker would win this case for his colleague and dear friend.

"I ... I have no idea what you are talking about?" Kim lied, remaining calm and collective. Norma and Jon sat with their hands enfolded.

"I remind you that you are under oath Mrs. Whaley, so I'll ask you again. Did you propose a ..." Steinbaker began once more.

Kim rudely curtailed his question, "I heard you the first time, and I *still* say that I have no knowledge of what you are talking about." Kim glanced nervously around the courtroom. Norma's friends must have somehow hurt Fredericko. That was the only explanation for this. What had they done to her Fredericko?

Steinbaker smirked at her smart remark. He then handed a thin sheet of paper to the judge, "Your honor, I submit this document which contains Mrs. Kim Whaley's signature to the court, item # 6." The judge took the paper, reviewed it carefully and nodded.

Steinbaker held the thin sheet in front of Kim's face so that she could clearly see the written signature, "Mrs. Whaley, I only care to ask you this once. Please don't waste any more of the court's time. Is this your written signature on this faxed document between you and Mr. Fredericko Mendoza, proposing a takeover between you two parties?"

Kim shook her head feverishly. Now, she was really concerned about Fredericko. Was there a chance that he had betrayed her for Norma? No, she could not let herself think of such things. She continued with her adamant denials, "No, I don't know what you are talking about!"

Steinbaker believed in the law and justice strongly. He could not believe how she could blatantly lie to the court. She gave him no choice but to resort to nastier measures.

"Your honor, I ask to play a tape as evidence, which was received anonymously ...."

"I object your honor, this evidence was not properly submitted and reviewed by the both sides," their lawyer began, giving Kim a perplexed look. Kim looked to her bewildered husband for support.

"Your honor, this tape is evidence that the witness' testimony is perjury," Steinbaker glanced to Jon and Norma. Jon nodded back.

"Objection overruled, I will allow this tape. May both attorneys' be advised, this is a case to settle whether a breach in a contractual agreement has occurred. No one is on trial here. The tape is admissible only if it can prove that a breach has occurred," the judge shook her head and adjusted her glasses.

The lawyer pushed down the button to play the tape, as a hush fell over the courtroom.

Kim's voice resonated from the recording, "I was thinking, someone with your influence and power could easily help me buy that share from Norma, and start a new company ...," the tape recanted as Kim buried her head in her hands.

"This would have to be a very, very secretive partnership.

You understand, don't you?" Kim's voice rang out as Jim's face turned several shades. He listened to his wife making this secret coalition. He looked from his lawyer to Kim for some explanation.

The tape continued, " ... with your money and influence, and my master deception, we could take Norma down ... I mean buy her out."

"I object! This tape has not been properly submitted and ..." Kim's lawyer vehemently rebuffed. It was too late. The tape had made the necessary point. Kim wanted to run in a corner and cry like a child. Mr. Steinbaker finally stopped the tape.

"Mrs. Whaley, are you telling us that you did not sign that paper, and that you did not make those statements now gathered in evidence?" Steinbaker stood pointing his finger to accuse, sweat dripping from his brow. He dared her with his eyes to deny it.

Everyone sat at the edge of their chairs, anxiously waiting for her response. Suddenly, the courtroom door flew open. Everyone turned to see Fredericko Mendoza waltz casually in.

Kim sighed with relief. Of course, he was there to save her! He had a plan. Her lover would rescue her, and take her away from all of these people. Kim looked puzzled, as Fredericko sat behind Norma and winked coolly at her.

What was he doing? Why was he sitting with the enemy?

"Mrs. Whaley?" Steinbaker persisted.

"No, I ... I," Kim said becoming unglued, her head nodding no, her hands shaking feverishly.

"Is this you on the tape? Did you propose a takeover? Was it not your intention to destroy the reputation of your employer and take a third of her company to start your own? Mrs. Whaley, you must answer. Did you ...?" he continued. His words became one blur of endless jargon. Kim struggled for words, her composure fading with each passing moment.

"I object, your honor, he is clearly badgering the witness!" Kim's lawyer proclaimed with no sympathy from the judge.

"Overruled, I want to hear her testimony," the judge said, enfolding her arms and waiting for a answer.

Suddenly, Kim went into a frenzy of denial. Her creamy complexioned face turned blood red, and tears streamed down her face. "No, I don't know what you're talking about! I ... No! ... No! Stop it! Stop!" she screamed as the courtroom murmuring reached it's height.

"Order! Order! This court will take a short ten minute recess in order that Mrs. Whaley can gather her thoughts," the judge said, as the bailiff helped her to chambers.

Kim immediately ran from the witness stand to Fredericko, and grabbed him as a child does its father, "Oh, Fredericko, you are here to save me! Please tell them they are all wrong. Please tell them about us. Tell them!" she cried earnestly with tears freely running down her cheeks.

Fredericko looked at her only with contempt now and shoved away her clutching hands. "Sorry, senora, but how do they say in La france, C'est la vie," he said, smiling and escorting Norma away. Jon walked by, shaking his head at her.

"No!" Kim screamed at him as he walked coldly away. Kim clutched at the air, as Jim peered on in utter shame at his wife's behavior. Kim looked at Norma, Jon, and Fredericko. They were all in league against her. She looked around the courtroom for some shred of support. Even Jim's bloodshot eyes turned away from her when she looked to him. They all seemed to be laughing at her defeat now. She hated them all. Kim could not believe it. She suddenly felt like that lonely, abandoned orphan that no one had wanted. She looked around just for a corner to crawl into.

She had thought Fredericko was her knight in shining armor. Chivalry had died with that sly, smirk, bastard! He had only used her.

Another man had used her. Kim let out a loud cry, right there in the middle of the courtroom. Jim went to her, and held her in his arms in spite of his own anger. Kim trembled with fear, feeling truly alone and dejected. Jim helped her to a seat, and rubbed her back until she stopped crying.

"Jim I, I ..." Kim began.

"Not now, you can explain it to me when we get home," Jim said in an angry tone he had never used before. He was so hurt, embarrassed, there were no simple words to explain his feelings at this moment. He had trusted this woman, and she had lied and deceived him. He had done this to so many women in his past, but he could never have imagined the pain could be this awful.

The court reconvened ten minutes later. Kim took the witness stand once again. This time, the judge asked Kim herself, "Is that your voice on the tape, Mrs. Whaley? Is this your signature?"

Kim finally answered yes to both embarrassing questions.

Next, came Fredericko's damning testimony. He nonchalantly recounted the events of their *entire* evening. Jim shook his head, as he realized what this man was saying about his wife. He had thought, how sweet of her for going through all that trouble on *their* special night. Yeah, all that trouble! Next, the hotel manager and room service, whom she had paid dearly for their discretion, testified against her, confirming Fredericko's testimony.

Then, came the testimony of Charles Brookton, who considered it his ultimate joy in life to see Kim Whaley gone from Ecstacy premises. He told the court that he had considered her trouble from the start, and had reported suspicious behavior to Norma Richmond.

Finally, *all thirty-five* of the models, who Kim had dared to testify, had their say on the witness stand. Kim could hardly bare this. All of her hard work in the last six months had been in vain. No one would ever trust her in New York or this town again, and her modeling career was already over. Norma had seen to that.

After what seemed endless hours of testimony, there was another short recess. There seemed to be endless chatter in the courtroom. Kim could not go near her husband or lawyer.

Everyone gave her looks of hatred and contempt, as she passed. She was soiled goods, having tried to destroy the reputation and business of the most respected woman in town.

She could hear the confusion outside, fans rallying for Norma, reporters, camera lights flashing. She just wanted it to all be over. The judge finally reappeared, and it was time to render her decision. The judge took her seat, as everyone settled in. She called the court to order and began, "No one is more excited to render a final decision for Richmond vs. Whaley, deciding whether there has been a breach of contract. This case has played more like a murder trial, and the press outside seemingly already has its verdict. Now," the judge put on her glasses to read the final decision, pausing to make just one more speech. She was becoming quite a ham due to all of the attention of the press.

Jon held on to Norma, kissing the crown of her head. Jim and Kim turned away from one another, both too hurt and angry to speak.

The judge began once more, "A year ago, when I rendered the decision in this divorce case, I felt that the decision made between the *two* parties were fair. However, this decision was made without the court's knowledge that Mr. Whaley had another marriage brewing on the kettle. Please, pardon my own use of vernacular here," she said letting out a little chuckle. She looked up and realized that no one was laughing with her. She cleared her throat and continued, "When the documents were drawn up by Ms. Richmond's ex-attorney, Jonathon Newman, the new Mrs. Whaley was generously included. This inclusion is the reason why we are here today. I have noted that Mr. Whaley had no prior knowledge of his wife's intentions. Nevertheless, the court has decided that there *has* been a breach of contract, and that the 30% profit share has been fully revoked," the courtroom was in an uproar with cheering and applause.

"Order! Order!" the judge yelled, "There will be no more outbursts. Please people, we are almost done here." The judge waited patiently for silence. She then continued, "Furthermore, both Jim and Kimberley Whaley will both resign their positions at Ecstacy Enterprises in New York City effective immediately. And next time, Mrs. Whaley ..." the judge said peering directly at Kim, "I advise you to honor your agreements more carefully, and not be so quick to renege on the promises you make to others. Court is adjourned!" the judge announced.

Hot tears trickled down Kim's face. Jim's head was still turned away from her. Kim turned her head just in time to see Fredericko congratulating Norma and Jon on their victory. He turned to wink at her. How could he? He had betrayed her. He never had any intention of helping her at all. Everyone surrounded Norma in love and victory. No one surrounded her in anything but contempt and hatred. She was just a joke, again. And after all of her hard work, for nothing!!!

"Kim, let's go home. You have got a hell of a lot of explaining to do!" Jim grabbed her arm, almost pushing her out of the chair. They walked quickly towards the door, reporters meeting them as they exited.

One reporter stepped in their path, as they headed towards the door, "How does it feel to find out your wife had an affair with another man in this court today?" Jim gave no response, but a cold, evil glare. The reporter backed away. As they left the courtroom, Kim turned towards Norma to give her one final hateful stare. Norma turned to catch a glance of it, and it sent a chill up her spine. Jon lovingly rubbed her side.

"What is it, love?" Jon said, turning to only see Kim's coat as she exited the courtroom.

"Don't let her spoil the mood. Let's go out to dinner. We'll make a night of it," Jon embraced her. He did not care who knew how much he loved this woman.

They had been seeing one another steadily for the last six months. They were taking it slow, very slow. Norma had so much hurt and anger to overcome when it came to Jim. She had really loved him. Jon knew that this was a milestone victory in helping her put behind the past, and move on with him. Jon understood her fears of being hurt again, and was being very patient with her. His affection and admiration grew for her daily. Her extraordinary strength and compassion fascinated him. He eyeballed her lengthy legs to her beautiful oval face. He hoped she wanted him as much as he wanted her.

"Look, we can have a candlelight dinner to celebrate. Sweetheart, we won! You won! Why do you look so worried?" Jon looked at Norma as she stared at the door where Kim had exited.

"I don't know Jon, I've just got this queer feeling. The look in that woman's eye. She hates me so much, she ..."

"That little airhead twit is just jealous of you. She is nothing for you to worry your head about. It's all over now. There is nothing more either one of them can do to you or us anymore," Jon tried reassuring her.

"Maybe you are right, I just can't shake this feeling, I ..."

"Madame, let me take you for de night on de town, wee? Come dit on? We will have de splendid time," Jon gave his poor imitation of a French accent. Candlelights and silky sheets danced in his heads. Six months was the longest he had ever waited for anyone. His whole body and manhood ached for Norma.

Norma laughed, "I hope the food is better than your fake accent."

They both laughed as they left the courtroom. A stream of relentless reporters greeted them at the door. Jon shielded Norma with his own body, as they safely passed through.

Norma lovingly glanced at Jon, shielding her from reporters, her Lancelot. She so wanted to thank him for supporting her through all of this madness. Maybe Jon was right. It was high time that she put behind her past, and give their relationship a real chance.

Jon had more than proven his love and loyalty, and he was more than worthy of her love. Besides, Jon was right. There was nothing more that either one of them could do to her. The nightmare was finally over.

* * *

"You made me look like a complete fool out there! I did not know what the hell was going on!" Jim shouted at the top of his lungs, slamming the door to their penthouse.

They had not spoken since before the five hour flight from Los Angeles to New York that afternoon. Jim had never been this angry at his wife since their marriage had begun.

"What were you thinking about, Kim? What were you thinking about? Now we have lost everything! Everything!" He yelled, as Kim plopped down on their black leather couch, attempting to soothe her throbbing head. She dared not speak. Maybe then he would stop yelling.

The phone rang, curtailing Jim's angry speech. Jim glared at her while answering the phone, "Hello ... yes ... yes ... okay man ... I gotcha ... goodbye," Jim hung up the phone. "Kim we have to finish this discussion later. I have to catch a flight out to Detroit. There's a guy there that owes me a couple of favors. He just might be able to lend us some money, and help us start our own company, over. Please ... try to stay clear of Norma while I'm gone. I don't know if I can handle anymore of your damn surprises," he grabbed the suitcase he had just put down. He then headed for the door once again. He looked up to see Kim sulking, those big, beautiful eyes filled with tears. Damn her. She was so beautiful, even now. He resisted the urge to take her in his arms, and kiss her passionately. "Be here when I get back!" was all he could get out. He slammed the door behind him.

Kim smiled at the slammed door, knowing that he was no longer angry. Her smile quickly turned to frantic rage, as she realized the full extent of what had happened in that courtroom today. She had lost everything! She had lost her title, the profits, and she had almost lost Jim. She screamed aloud in exasperation. Her plan had failed.

Kim allowed herself to fall to the carpet indulging in her own self pity. She beat her fists hard on the carpet, kicking in frustration. She then lay there for the space of an hour, still, silent, not knowing what to say or do anymore. She sat still so long, her bones became stiff. Finally, she pushed herself back up to the couch.

A plan of action finally emerged, as she frantically scuffled from the couch to her purse on the dining room chair. She emptied the contents of her purse on to the floor. She had to find Fredericko's number. She knew she had scribbled it on a paper napkin at that party. She knew it had to be there. Kim frowned as she touched something wet and gushy on her hand.

Kim kneeled on the floor, determined to complete her search. A pink, soft napkin finally emerged. Ah! there it was! She held the napkin as if it were pure gold. She looked at the number carefully, repeating it in her mind until she reached the phone in the hall. She picked up the phone, her hands shaking and lips quivering uncontrollably.

He would have to explain it to her now! There had to be some reason why he would betray her like this. He could not just make love to her like that and walk away, not if she had anything to say about it. She dialed the number only to discover that it was now disconnected.

Kim angrily shoved the dining room table, destroying the vase full of flowers that sat upon it as it tumbled to the hardwood floor surrounding it. She sat there on the floor again, crying in the dark—alone, confused, hopeless and desperate. She was broken just like that vase.

Every thought that came into her head centered on what the next move should be. How could she possibly get past this one? After all, Norma had won back everything. She had overcome every hurdle Kim had ever attempted to put before her.

She felt as if she were in the bottom of a deep, dark pit, and could not see her way out.

Another idea came, and she rushed to the phone once more. Norma, that's it! She would call Norma, maybe blackmail her, something! There had to be a way to redeem herself. Norma could not win this fight. She again picked up the phone. It rang several times, and then a sleepy Norma picked up the phone, "Hello ... hello ... hello," Norma said nervously by the third try.

Kim hung up the phone and then threw it against her front door. The beeping of it made her head hurt. Norma had won, there was no use. Kim screamed with all of her might and dug her nails and head into the floor, scratching and crawling around in the dark like a small animal. All of her life she had to fight for everything she had ever wanted. She was tired of fighting. She imagined a large brick wall, and there she was beating her bare hands against the hard brick wall, her hands all bloody. Oh, how Kim wished she could just die, right this minute. What was the use in living now?

Norma had practically thrown her out in the street. Why did people like Norma always get everything, and she end up with nothing! She could not work in anyone's company. Who would trust her? She could never work as a model again, and make a living, Norma had seen to that. What was there for her to do? And Jim, well he would eventually get tired of her, too.

She rushed to her bathroom cabinet and emptied all of the contents: Ibuprofen, Nuprin, Excedrin, and a bottle of prescription sleeping pills she had been given after her supposed miscarriage. There was nothing left for her to do. She would just kill herself.

Kim spread the pills all over the bathroom counter, and tried to peer deep into her own face and eyes in the mirror. She could hardly see her own reflection through the tears. She took the handful of pills, and held them to her mouth, her whole body shaking in desperation and anguish. She dropped a few, and bent down to pick them up. Kim's eyes widened in full horror, as she realized what she was actually about to do.

"Why should I kill myself? She is the one causing all of the pain," she thought aloud. The pills dropped like raindrops from her hands on to the floor. After all, Norma Richmond was the source of all her misery. She was the reason why she had lost everything. She was the reason why Fredericko had been disloyal. *She* was the one that should go. Why not just kill her?

Kim suddenly felt a strange new maddening energy emerge within her. It was like she had come back to life again. She quickly got the broom, and swept up the mess she had made in her bathroom. Kim was ashamed of herself for what she had been thinking. She washed her tear-stricken face, and combed her disheveled hair.

"Hmmmm," Kim smiled in the mirror, and sang her mother's old rocking chair song. "Thank you, Mommy for saving me," Kim said closing her eyes and seeing her mother's face, tears freely flowing.

Kim opened her eyes again to behold strange visions in the bathroom mirror. There she was as a little girl, pigtails and all, her mother standing right beside her. Her mommy was alive and well, loving her, comforting her. Kim reached out for her reflection, closing her eyes and breathing in deep. She could smell her mother's old perfume, it was something like daffodils touched with a gentle rain on a new spring day. How she loved that smell.

Kim opened her eyes once again. Her hands were still extended, but she was now standing alone. Her mother had been the only one that she had ever loved. She had been gone for so very long now. No one else mattered. Nothing else mattered, and now that bitch Norma had to go.

Norma sat in front of her vanity table mirror. She was wearing a towel over her head and body, and a thick clay mask on her face, when the phone rang.

"Oh, no, not this again!" Norma frowned. She had been receiving strange phone calls all hours of the day and night. The creep would never say anything, just hold the phone. Guess she would have to change her number again.

"Hello, is this Ms. Norma Richmond?" the mysterious voice inquired.

"Yes, may I ask who's calling?" Norma laughed a little, looking at her face with all that gook on it.

"This is Michelle Windom from the People's Choice Awards. Every year we select from our finest citizens. These are people who we feel have really made a difference. This year's awards show is particularly significant, since it is the first of one of the new millennium. This year the focus is on people who have made a difference in the last decade. Your name was one of the first on our list. *Essence* and *Ebony* have both carried your story ... it is quite fascinating Ms. Richmond ...," she said, as Norma grinned.

"Yes, well ...," Norma began her speech of modesty.

"The People's Choice Award would like to honor you this season for being a trailblazer for women in the field of modeling," the speaker began.

Norma was absolutely speechless. She wanted to pinch herself, to see if she was dreaming.

"Ms. Richmond? Are you still there? Ms. Richmond ..." Ms. Windom anxiously awaited Norma's response.

"I am so ... so thrilled ... I don't know what to say ... I," Norma was almost ready to scream from sheer excitement. She had not felt this good since the first day she stepped into her office at Ecstacy.

"Just say yes. The ceremonies will be held on March 12th this year at the Shrine Auditorium. I am sorry for notifying you so late, but you are a woman that's very hard to get in touch with. We have tried to leave messages and e-mail. We will provide limousine services for you and a guest to and from the awards. The awards also include a private dinner before, and party afterwards. It will be a special night to remember, and the show will provide complementary tickets to up to four guests," she explained.

"Well, yes, yes, yes! I am so excited. I feel a little like Cinderella ... Cinderella Brown that is," Norma bubbled with happiness.

"I will be contacting you by address and e-mail, Ms. Richmond with more details," Windom smiled at Norma's sincere gratitude. What a great lady!

Norma hung up the phone, and let out exuberant screams around the house. She then put in a call to both of her sisters, and told them she would make the arrangements for them to attend. It would be a good time for she and Flora to reunite after all of these years.

Norma stood in the middle of her kitchen looking in horror at the calendar. It was already the middle of February, and she now had to prepare. There was the dress, her hair, and, "Jon, I've got to tell, Jon ..." she said, just as he peeked through the open front door.

"Forgot to tell me what? You know Norma, it's dangerous leaving your door open like that. A prowler could walk in," he said, shutting the door and turning to face her. He jumped back a little when he did see her.

"Oh, Jon, I ..." Norma stopped short as she realized she was standing there half-naked with a towel on her body and head, and a grotesque mask on her face. Jon resisted the urge to laugh at her obvious embarrassment. She had forgotten all about their lunch date today in her excitement.

Norma broke the ice, and burst out in laughter. Jon followed her lead. They stood there laughing so hard, until they were completely out of breath.

"So, what is it you wanted to tell me, cookie monster?" he said, tears welling in his eyes from all of the laughter. She playfully tapped him.

"The awards show called ... and we've got a limo ... and I don't have a dress yet ... and I ..."

"Woh, slow it down. Now what happened?" Jon encouraged her to breathe in deep and calm down.

"The People's Choice Awards show called, and they are going to honor me with a prestigious award. And of course, I wanted to know if you could escort me? It's in March?" Norma made her way to the bathroom to wash her clay-drenched face.

"Oh, let me check my schedule for March," Jon kidded putting his hand on his brow, as if he were contemplating. He then smiled and answered, "Woman, of course I can go. I wouldn't miss it for the world." He liked the sense of humor they now shared, as they became more comfortable with one another.

A look of desire settled on his face, when he realized that the woman he wanted more than anything was standing there half-naked.

"Would you like some help with that?" he stood there watching intensely, as she washed her face with warm water. The deep beautiful brown of her skin finally emerged as the clay dissolved.

"No thank you, Mr. Fixit," she said, taking the washcloth he had in his hand from him and tapping him lightly in the face. Norma ran up the stairs as he chased her playfully.

"Watch out my lady, I'm a comin' for ya," Jon ran up the stairs to catch her.

Chapter
14

The Ball

"You will not be sorry, Russell," Jim said shaking, his old friend's hand. They were seated in a Detroit restaurant, just north of Woodward street. The waiter brought the check, as Jim gathered his briefcase and coat. It had been a week and a half of wheeling and dealing with this man.

"I had better *not* be. You tell your wife that there will be no more crazy antics," Russell said, giving him a look of admonishment. Russell reached for the bill, but Jim would not have it.

"Look, I got the check, man," Jim said, gratitude in his eyes. He had come through for him.

Russell Warner gave Jim no argument. He had just written Jim a loan check for a quarter of a million dollars. Jim would use it to finance a new modeling agency for he and Kim. They would start anew.

"Look man, I've got it all under control," Jim said his good-byes to his long time friend and made his way to a pay phone to tell his wife the good news. He had made the local hotel his home, and was now ready to get back to his own. He had just made the hustle of his life. Jim smiled, as he imagined his wife's reaction. He had had plenty of time for his anger to cool. He was now hungry for Kim. He had been way too hard on her. After all, they were two of a kind. He could not blame her for what she was.

The phone rang and rang, no answer. He remembered how strangely calm she had seemed the last time he had called her from his hotel. He knew her well enough to know that something was going on. Jim grew more impatient with each ring. Ah! Kim was probably sore at him for being gone so long. He would solve all of that when he arrived home.

He could hardly wait to tell her. Maybe this would finally give her the happiness that she was seeking. Maybe it was just the thing that she needed to forget about her stupid vendetta against Norma, and concentrate on having a family. He never understood why she hated Norma so much. Now they would have their own company, without Norma Richmond.

After letting the phone ring about ten times, Jim finally decided to hang up. Oh, no bother, he would surprise her with champagne and flowers. Jim hurried to make his flight reservations for home.

"What color would you like, Ms.?" the young girl in the wig shop said as Kim squinted her face in indecision.

"Black, and short. I want to see what its like to wear a shorter style. My husband has been begging me to cut my hair for years. I just can't find the heart," Kim said with a fake southern accent tone. The girl disappeared into a small curtain behind the counter.

Kim tapped her fingers on the counter, hoping the girl would appear soon with what she had asked. Out of sheer boredom, she peered up at the small television set above the counter, and listened to the newscaster.

"The People's Choice Awards will be honoring Norma Richmond, the modeling guru of the past decade, along with a hosts of other celebrities at their ceremonies this week at the Shrine Auditorium in Los Angeles ..."

The other words blurred as the girl brought out a short bob-styled wig. Kim hated it, but told her it was fine. She paid her cash. She glanced at her watch impatiently. The girl stuffed the wig into a small brown paper bag, and handed it to her. She had to hurry. She had to make good time.

Norma turned around in the mirror, and carefully scanned every inch of her lean body through her sheer black slip. Every eye would be on her tonight. She had to look especially beautiful not only for them, but for herself and Jon as well. She wondered if she had been too short with him earlier, practically ordering him over at six-thirty. Her eyes wandered over to the clock, 5:55, she had to move faster. She reached over to pick up the box containing her dress.

Norma had called in a favor to her favorite European designer, Pierre Du Pont, the day after she had received the call. She smoothed her hands over the tall box, smiling with adulation. She then took a tall pair of scissors and cut the thick tape, opening the box. Her fingers shook with anticipation, much like that of a child at Christmas opening her presents. She threw the endless streams of wrapping paper to the floor in search of her dress. Finally, Norma beheld her dress. It was exquisite. She gently lifted the dress out of the box, letting out a sigh of pure joy.

The gown was a deep purple velvet, slightly trimmed with traces of golden thread at its sides, tiny spaghetti straps touching her shoulders. Norma felt up and down the velvet material, feeling her clothes for quality and authenticity. She spread the dress over her body and pondered her image in the full body mirror.

The dress was floor length, cut low in the front to accentuate her bustline. It was cut to fit perfectly at her small waist. The split on its side would reveal her ebony legs, but would not destroy the mystique of her look. Pierre had done marvelously this time. It was exactly the way she had pictured it.

Norma carefully examined the long black gloves, black shawl, and black pumps to go with her dress, placed neatly on her king size bed. Her matching diamond necklace and earrings would fit in perfectly with this evening's attire. Norma held up her dress, and spun around completely once. She was so happy she could burst inside.

Momma would have been so proud. Here her baby was being honored tonight. Her two sisters would be there to support her, along with celebrity friends, and a plethora of models. Juanita had called earlier to let her know that she and Flora had arrived in town safely. Everything would be perfect. It would be her night.

Norma almost fell over backwards as she slipped into her beautiful gown, feet first. She sighed aloud, took a deep breath, and gently pulled the dress up her tall, lean physique. She then whirled around her black shawl, and placed it on as well.

Norma practiced facial expressions, and several poses in her vanity mirror. It was something she had done frequently in the early days to prepare for a shoot.

Norma's life and accomplishments passed before her eyes, as she contemplated her reflection in the mirror. Tears mixed with joy and past pain filled her eyes. She never could have imagined all those years ago in New York, that her journey would take her to this point. All the work, all the pain, the disappointment, and rejection seemed so far away. It all seemed worth it now. Her eyes glanced over to the clock, 6:15. She had to get a move on.

Norma did a quick check of her make-up and hair, which had been done earlier that afternoon by her old friend Brenda. Her jet black hair was swept up in an elaborate ball on her head, tiny flattering curls surrounding her beautiful oval face. She looked much like a fairy princess going to her ball, yes, Cinderella Brown.

"My gal, lak a purty baby doll," Marie would have said. Norma closed her eyes, smiling as she imagined her mother's warm embrace. A sense of loss overtook her, and a tear trickled down her face. Norma held out her arms for a mother's touch. That touch that never came.

Norma gently wiped her tear away, and shook herself back to reality. It was times like this when she missed her mother the most. She would have given away all of her fame and money in the world, just to hear her mother's voice and see her face again. Suddenly, a strange chill rushed in from her bedroom window. "Mama," Norma called out, but laughed to herself as she saw that it was just the window slightly opened, the cold air seeping in. Norma rushed over to close the window. Funny, she could not remember having opened it.

Norma's thoughts shifted to Juanita and Flora. They were probably preparing for tonight as well. So, in a sense, mama would be there, through all of them, there together. They would all celebrate afterwards, maybe with their own special dinner. It would be the first time that the three of them had been together since the funeral.

She was also glad that peace had been made with Flora. Hate was too draining of an energy. She had learned that, if nothing else, from Kimberley. That poor soul. She wondered what she was doing now.

Norma had barely slipped her feet into her pumps, when the doorbell rang. Six-thirty, that Jon, right on time. She liked that about him, amongst many things.

"May I inquire what a pretty little lady like you wants with a big gun like that?" the portly vendor said to Kim, in a patronizing tone.

"Look sir, I don't have a lot of time. I ... just give me *that!*" Kim pointed to a thirty-eight caliber pistol.

"Well, uh ma'am there's a thirty day waiting period that ... uh," the vendor began, as Kim pulled out a couple of hundreds. His eyes widened, as he peered on. She finally stopped and looked up at him.

"Okay, right up an' comin'. But a fine thang like you don't look like she could hurt a fly," he continued, as Kim smiled, handing him the cash. Kim rushed outside to wait for the taxi she had called, breathing in the unfamiliar smells and foreign air.

"Kim honey," Jim burst open the door to their New York penthouse to find it empty, and in a complete mess. Kim had left in a hurry, papers and clothes everywhere.

"I guess somebody left in a hurry," Jim thought aloud, putting down the champagne glass and flowers and sinking into their black leather couch. A beeping sound called his attention to the phone, very apparently off the hook. Jim slammed the phone on its receiver. He had planned a romantic evening. He had hoped it would be a new beginning. He loved Kim so much.

Jim noticed scribbling on some yellow-lined paper. He almost threw it away, until Kim's handwriting caught his attention. It read: Flight #: 2146 to Los Angeles. Now what would ...? He did not even want to know. Jim popped open the $200 bottle of champagne and retired for the evening.

Norma turned around to examine herself one last time in the dining room mirror, before taking a serious inhale. She finally opened the door. Jon stood like a vision of an angel before her. Norma was taken aback, "Oh, Jon," she said perusing him from head to toe. His white tux with its purple bow tie suited her perfectly.

"I hope that means you like it. I almost had to cut this myself," Jon ran his fingers through the top of his silky black hair and smiling. He was so amazing.

Norma truly felt like a princess, as she beheld the shiny black stretch limousine in the driveway. A driver stood ready to serve them upon request.

"Shall we, my dear?" Jon stretched out his helping hand to help her down the three marble steps.

"Thank you, sir," she obliged him. Jon entangled his arm gently around hers, giving her a long luscious look as they approached the limo. He took one finger, and gently touched her perfectly soft and pursing lips. Norma gently kissed his finger, and smiled big.

He wanted her, and could see that she finally wanted him the same way. His eyes wandered up and down her body as if they were hands touching and feeling every part of her. He knew that she did not have to say one word. It was written all over her face. Beautiful, was a word which lacked the significance to describe her elegance and shining beauty in this precious moment.

Norma motioned to open her own door, when Jon stopped her.

"No, *you* are the queen of the night, and the queen of my heart," Jon opened the door for her. He usually allowed her to fully express her need for independence, but tonight he would pamper her. She certainly deserved it after all that she had been through.

Norma stepped back, and allowed him to be the perfect gentleman, opening the limo door and helping her inside.

"Well, aren't I the lucky one," Norma said as she sat inside the limo. Norma sighed with relief and thought, " Chivalry is not dead, after all."

"It's your night," Jon closed her door and rushed to his own side. The driver waited for Jon's signal to proceed.

Norma blushed all over, feeling all warm inside. She sensed that tonight would be *their* night as well. As they were driven to the auditorium, lust pervaded like a cloud, as if impregnated with the rainfall of a new season. It came and stood in the midst of a friendship that had already grown into love, making its stay and urge more tangible and harder to resist. Lust came as the new budding flowers of springtime waiting to spread after a long, cold winter. Love and lust combined in a sensual mix over them both, as they listened to romantic music, sipped on champagne, and watched nothing but the brown of each other's eyes. Eros was sitting on the napes of their necks, and on their love.

"We're here," the chauffeur said, startling both Norma and Jonathon, as their minds wandered from other erotic places.

Jon finally broke the silence, "I guess it's time to show them all, Norma Jeanette," he gently grabbed her hand and squeezed it.

Norma smiled and turned her body as the door was opened to a madhouse of reporters and fans. Norma suddenly felt like a sardine in a can, confined and carefully scrutinized. She squeezed Jon's hand back, and looked for a familiar face in the crowd.

Her eyes focused on the red carpet just below her black pumps, leading to the auditorium. Jon held out his hand to help her out of the limo. The fans went absolutely mad. Reporters came left and right, lights flashed from every direction. Norma was in awe. I mean, she was no movie star. She had been out of the real limelight for years, having made the behind the scene switch many years previously. She had forgotten how nervous that part of it all made her. Except for a few crazy reports and tabloid reporters that followed her marital affairs, the press had left her in peace. They usually operated on her terms. Now she felt much like their victim, picked, prodded and examined.

"How does it feel to be in the limelight once more, Ms. Richmond?" the reporter inquired.

"Well ah ... great! I just never realized how popular I was again ... I don't know, it just feels so ... so ... all of a sudden," Norma nodded to Jon that it was the only question that she intended to answer.

Jon grabbed her hand, and led her towards the large auditorium door. Jon, her love, her protector. She sighed with a new kind of calmness and peace. Inside, there would be family, friends, colleagues and *her* girls. A few teenagers screamed, and Norma turned to observe all of the racket. She and Jon turned to face Fredericko, pulling up in a black Porsche, a tan girl with waist length hair at his side. That Fredericko! She waved and sighed with relief, finally someone familiar. Another flash of light from a photographer's camera blazed in her eyes. Norma slowly panned her eyes down to the red carpet leading to the large golden door, open, waiting for her grand entrance.

"Norma are you okay. You look so frightened," Jon smoothed his hand against the small of her back.

Norma looked in his eyes for reassurance. She felt so small and pathetic. She needed his strength now. She had always had to be so strong for herself and everyone else. It felt so nice to have this wonderful soul beside her, protecting her, loving her.

Jon held up her chin, as they stopped just in front of the door.

"Look up beautiful, its time to shine like the star you are. I will be here to catch you if you fall," Jon said lovingly, never breaking his glance from her eyes. Norma's eyes welled with tears. For now, she finally understood the true meaning of ecstasy.

Ecstasy, it was not the company, money, or success. It was having faith in God and family, she had learned that first from Mama, then from Juanita again. Ecstasy, it was also having a true soul mate, someone that felt you and truly made you feel so loved. She realized too, that it was by achieving her goals: the company, success, and money that had given her the courage to accept his love. It had been a long journey, but now she finally felt at home.

Norma smiled through the tears which welled in her eyes, tears of happiness and pure appreciation. She turned and waved to the voracious crowd once more. She held tightly to what she estimated as her greatest treasure, her Jon. He gave her a slight kiss as they edged closer towards *the* door. Lights flashed again, no doubt capturing one of tomorrow's headlines. Norma sighed with contentment and sheer joy of the moment.

Norma and Jon took one more look in each other's eyes, before stepping inside. The door, to the Shrine, *now* represented a place where she would finally be recognized for her hard work and achievements in an industry which had rejected her bitterly in the early years. Funny, how it did not matter so much now. There was no anger, no bitterness, only gratitude and joy. It was all good!

An awful scream rang out from the crowd, "She's got a gun!" someone yelled. Norma looked around frantically, as Jon held her down and tried to push her inside the door. Suddenly, a firecracker like sound went off twice. Norma suddenly felt a sharp pain, as the salty taste of blood filled her mouth. Jon held her close, never losing her eyes, as blood gushed out from her head. Jon looked at his hands, now filled with Norma's dripping blood, his lips quivering in disbelief.

"No! Somebody help! Aw ... God no!" Jon screamed, tears filling his eyes. The crowd ran in every direction, the sounds of police sirens and an ambulance a short distance away.

Norma whispered weakly, "Jon," as Jon cuddled her in his arms, her body descending lifelessly towards the ground. Norma reached out for Jon's hands once more, and then it all went black.

Kim ran away quickly as everyone rushed to Norma's side. There were screams and all sorts of commotion. It was easy to make a get away with all of the confusion around her. She wished she could have shot her again, but there was just no way. Jon was in her way! Damn him!

She dumped the wig and gloves in a near by trash can, and blended with the crowd until she reached a small Chinese restaurant. Los Angeles suddenly seemed so far from her New York home.

Kim rushed inside the restaurant, walking swiftly until she reached the restroom in the back. She rushed inside a stall to change her clothes, and allow traffic outside to die down. If she just waited there a few moments, everything would be fine. She heard the sirens gathering outside, the police, the ambulance.

She waited there in the stall, as two ladies discussed the event in the restroom. She smiled to herself proudly. At least, she had accomplished what she had set out to do.

Kim waited at least twenty minutes. She made sure no one else was in the restroom, before finally emerging from her stall. Kim stared intently at herself in the mirror. She hardly recognized herself. A little sweat was dripping from her brow, her hair wrapped in a tight bun in the back of her head because of the wig. Her head was beginning to hurt from the tight knot at the back.

Kim stared at herself a while, grateful that no one had recognized her. She smiled to herself, but her smile turned to a slight frown. An uncommon surge of guilt swept over her. She held up the hands that had done this deed, and examined them closely. Tears welled up in her eyes, tears that she was unable to explain. She had thought herself freed of emotion after that night on the floor in her penthouse. Up to this point, she had felt so hallow and empty inside. It was as if someone else had done this thing, and here she was just returning. What was there to feel guilty about? She hated Norma, anyway.

"Oh, well, it's done now," she said aloud, shrugging her shoulders. She took one last look, and then proceeded out of the restroom. She had to hurry to catch her plane.

Chapter 15

Revelations

Jim awoke to a horrible hangover after a night of champagne and television. He was bent over the bathroom stool, when he heard the door slam. Jim stumbled into the living room to meet his wife, who was now domestically making a pot of coffee.

"Rough night, Jim dear ... eh ...," Kim said nonchalantly.

"Where in the hell have you been? I bought some champagne for us and ..." Jim began.

"And I can see that you got started without me," Kim said batting her eyes and looking at him sarcastically.

"Why do you have to be such a ...?" Jim roughly grabbed Kim, intending to shake her. He gave in to the urge to kiss her instead. He had missed her so. He had stayed away way too long. What the heck? They could make up for lost time now.

"Hey, why don't we go and make up? I have good news Kimberley babe, I got a new partner and I can give you all the power *you* want, I ..." Kim coldly pushed him away.

Jim stopped short, watching his wife walk apathetically away. He had never seen this mood before. It sort of turned him on. Maybe this would be one of her kinky games. He could hardly wait to ravage her again. Kim continued ignoring her husband, and began gathering her clothes from their bedroom, instead.

"Kim, what are you doing? Did you hear what I said? I ..." Jim began again.

"Yes, I heard you. And I hope that makes you happy," Kim took her suitcase from their closet.

Jim could not believe his eyes and ears. Why walk out now? What more did she want? He would do or say *anything* just to make her stay.

"Make me happy? I *thought* this would make *you* happy, too. I've been in meetings all week, because I thought ... thought that ..." Jim's head was still pounding from last night's adventures. It was hard to concentrate, but he would say whatever she needed to hear.

Kim turned around and eyed him with a bitter coldness that he had never seen before. Jim backed away a bit. "Hey, it's really been fun baby, but I gotta split," Kim said, no feeling in her voice or eyes.

There was no more need for pretenses. He had served his purpose. He had helped her all that he could. She now looked at what once was a beautifully crafted man. At one time, they even had a lot in common. Now he stood before her weak, begging and of no use to her now. He was pathetic.

"What in the hell do you mean, woman? You can't just walk away like this. I can give you anything, anything you want. I know it hasn't been easy lately, okay ... I should never have left like that! I should have called! Well ... what! What do you want me to say?" Jim begged, as Kim emptied out the rest of her drawers, throwing handfuls of items into her bags. Jim attempted to stop her, unsuccessfully. He removed clothes from the suitcase, as she placed them in. Kim sighed in exasperation. Jim finally stopped, when he realized that she was intent on leaving. There was nothing he could say or do about it. A lump grew in his throat, and the sickening feeling in his stomach became more intense.

Kim finished her quick packing, finally zipping up her suitcase and pulling in the small duffel bag which she had stuffed to the top. "I'll send for the rest of my things," Kim stared at the front door.

Jim stood there speechless, helpless. This had never happened to him before. No woman had ever dared to leave him like this, for no reason. He had always been the one to say when and if it was over. He could not let her do this to him.

Kim made her final lunge towards the door, as Jim made his desperate, final plea, "But Kim … Kim baby … baby I LOVE YOU," he said half crying, his head feeling as if it was about to explode. He had never been more sincere about anything in his life. This all seemed a surreal nightmare.

Kim stopped when he said this, and pondered this for a moment. Jim sighed with relief, thinking that he had touched on some emotion within this woman, this stranger he had called his wife up until now. Kim placed her things down for a moment.

Kim stared at Jim with a strange scowl in her brow. She contemplated. She knew that even if he loved her now, he could never love her forever. No man ever had, and ever could. Funny she had lived for hate so long, that love was too much of a stranger to invite in.

She turned sideways towards her husband, and examined him intently. This man, almost to his knees begging her to stay, had nothing in his eyes but pure love and hope. She almost wanted to dive in and swim in this love, but she resisted. It was time to be strong. She did not need his love. She needed no one.

Kim stood straight, posed and composed as she spoke with ease, "But you see Jim. I do not love you … I NEVER did. I only wanted to hurt Norma. I'm so sorry that I hurt you, too. Our time is over, and I must go now." Kim once again picked up her things and opened the door. This time, Jim dared not interfere. They had both said all they needed to say.

Jim was broken. He watched the only woman he had ever loved walk out of the door. He realized that there was nothing he could have done to make her stay, "Well to HELL with you, then! You … you bitch!" he yelled, hurling her favorite statuette towards the door. Kim had already shut the door. A small fragment of the statuette broke, as it crashed against the door and to the carpet. Jim stumbled a bit, and sank into the black leather couch. He cradled his body in pain, and wept like a new born babe.

"Norma ... love, can you hear me?" Jon whispered, as Norma batted her blurry eyes. It took a while to adjust to the light, but Jon's image finally became clearer.

"What ... what happened ...? Where am I?" Norma asked, feeling a horrible pain shoot up her arms. As her vision cleared, Jon's face came into focus. Norma felt calmed by his presence.

"Sweetheart, you're in the hospital ... Cedar Sinai ... your head was grazed by a bullet. One inch closer and God help us all. You are one lucky lady," Jon smiled as Norma frowned and scratched the side of her head.

"Lucky, huh!" Norma tried raising her head. It was no use, the pain was too great. She gasped, and reclined back.

"No, don't move," Jon hovering at her side. "You are finally going to get those few weeks of rest I've been urging you to take. Juanita is outside waiting to see you. She has a few of her church members outside, and they are all praying for you."

Norma smiled inside. She had so much admiration for her sister. She always knew the right things to say and do. She was so proud of her, as Mama would have been. She truly held up the light for the family. Speaking of family, she wondered if Flora was outside as well.

"Flora?" Norma was anxious to see her baby sister again.

"Yes, but you can see them all later, you must try to rest now," Jon gently rubbed her hand.

"Rest ... Jon what happened? The last thing I remember ... we were standing by the ...."

"It was Kim, Norma, she tried to kill you," Jon blurted out.

"Kill me, but ..."

"Norma, the police found a wig and gloves in the trash can alley. A witness saw her take it off and disappear into the crowd. The woman's description fit Kim perfectly. She was also identified by both the wig and gun shop owners, and her flight reservation was easy to figure out. How many Kimberley Richmond's do you think there were on last night's flight to New York from Los Angeles? The woman is not only crazy, she's just not very smart and sloppy, too."

"But she hated me that much ...." Norma stumbled from pain both inside and out. "But why? She has Jim, she even had 30% of my company until she screwed that up ... Did it mean that much to her? I just ... just don't understand? What more? Did Jim put her up to this?" Norma tried raising her body once more, but collapsed again in pain.

"Sweetheart just rest. All of your questions will be answered later. The authorities are on their way to New York as we speak," Jon gently kissed her forehead.

Norma could no longer resist the temptation to sleep, "Later, I ... will know ... know later," she mumbled, her eyes involuntarily closing.

Jon waited for her to relax completely. He lovingly stroked the top of her head, and smiled. He waited patiently for her to fall asleep, before finally leaving her side.

It was 2:30 p.m. when the police frantically knocked on the door to the Whaleys' Manhattan penthouse. Jim thought he was dreaming at first when he heard the loud knock at the door. The strong smell of gin had seemingly sunk beneath his flesh, and it bothered his own nostrils. He had not stopped drinking since Kim had left that morning.

Jim stumbled, but finally made his way to the door to four men, two police officers and two men in suits.

"Hello, Mr. Whaley, my name is Sergeant Cameron and we have a search warrant. We are here to investigate ..." the police officer said, flashing his badge. He turned his face away coughing, the gin aroma from Jim being so strong.

Jim was too intoxicated to put up a front. An officer pushed pass him, and began searching his home.

"Wai ... a minute ... you can ... jus ..." Jim began, but could not quite get the rest out.

"Mr. Whaley, can you verify your whereabouts last night? Were you in Los Angeles last night?" another officer took over for the sergeant.

"What, I 'ave been here I ... whats dhis abou?" Jim managed to get out, his vision now as unstable as his speech and motor ability.

"Mr. Whaley, have you seen this morning's paper? There was an attempt on your ex-wife's life at an awards show at the Shrine Auditorium. She was one of the honorees. We have reason to believe that your current wife was involved with last night's shooting. Have you spoken to your wife since last night, Mr. Whaley?" the officer continued. Jim was finally assisted to a chair, because of his instability. It was obvious that he had no idea what they were talking about.

"Look what I found Jack ...." Sergeant Cameron came out with black glasses and a black coat. "I also found fibers of hair inside. Does that poor S.O.B even know what the hell is goin' on here" the officer inquired as the other officers shook their heads.

"Look Mr. Whaley, I don't suppose you know where your wife is now, eh?" another officer asked as Jim shook his head.

"Why don't you sober up and come down to the station tonight. We'll leave you to ... uh ... whatever ... just come straight to the station when you are up to it. Don't let us have to come and get you," one officer said as they all seemed to advance to the door together on cue.

"Oh, and Mr. Whaley, I wouldn't even think of leaving town if I were you," Sergeant Cameron said, the other officers filing out of the door. Jim sat there not quite fully aware of what was going on, as they finally slammed the door and left him in his misery.

* * *

Robert Bailey sat in a Beverly Hills Norms, eyeing his watch. He was the toughest private eye this side of Hollywood. He had worked for the L.A.P.D. for twenty years before retiring and becoming a private investigator. He had seen so much violence those twenty years with the force. He needed a change. It was a chance to get away from the danger. Besides, most of the time he had only worked for rich husbands or wives who wanted to catch their spouses cheating. When Jonathon Newman called with such a high profile case, he wanted in on the action. This was a chance to enhance his clientele.

He was glancing at his watch again, when Jon swung the door of the restaurant open. He searched around, breathless from running in from the parking lot. His eyes finally settled on a plump Caucasian man chewing on some ice. He waved a little, and Bailey lifted his eyebrows. Jon sat in the chair directly across from him.

"Hey man, I was thinkin' you was gonna stand me up," Bailey said with a devilish grin.

"So what gives, you got the goods on Kim Whaley?" Jon replied, anxious to know himself why Kim hated a woman he loved so much.

"Hey, hold on to your horses, lover boy. I've got it right here," Bailey pulled out a manilla folder. He opened it to read the information inside. "Okay let's see here. Turns out that Kim has been an orphan since the age of twelve. She ran away when she was fifteen because of alleged rape by one of her foster parents."

"Man, I know all of that from the basic background check we did on her, when she first came to Ecstacy. Have you got anything else?" Jon said, very impatiently.

"But here is something I bet you didn't know," he pulled out a picture of what appeared to be a very fair-skinned, attractive, but elderly woman.

171

"What?" Jon looked at the picture confused.

"Kimberley Brandon was born to a Jessica Brandon twenty miles outside of Maryland. Jessica had an affair with Joseph Richmond."

"Norma's father? But who's to say that ..."

"Thought you'd ask, so here's the birth certificate, right here," Bailey pulled out an authentic birth certificate for Jon to view. Sure enough, Joseph Richmond was listed as the birth father for Kimberley Brandon.

Jon looked at it in shock, "My God! that makes Kim ..."

"At least thirty-four years old. But since when is it a crime for a woman to falsify her age, eh?" Bailey laughed.

Jon rolled his eyes. This was no laughing matter. The detective continued, "The affair continued until Kim was at least ten years old. Apparently, Mrs. Richmond got wind of it, and the affair ended shortly thereafter. Folks in that town say Jessica Brandon lost her mind after that, leaving her ten year old daughter to care for herself. She died of a broken heart at forty-seven," Bailey took a sip of coffee.

"This woman was forty-seven?" Jon said amazed. He thought the woman in the picture at least sixty.

"Yeah, ain't love grand?" Bailey began, but stopped quickly realizing that his sense of humor was not very appealing to Jon in this matter.

"Her sister, of course, now it all makes sense," Jon said scratching his chin.

Kim had never wanted the modeling career, that was just icing on the cake. She never even wanted Jim. This was only about revenge; revenge for her mother's death; revenge for the years of abuse; revenge for the lost of a father. She blamed Norma and her mother for it all.

"Of course, she blames Norma for taking her mother away, and making her an orphan," Jon finally said aloud, feeling as if a light bulb had gone off in his head.

The detective continued, "Oh, and it gets more juicy than that. Apparently, there was a Kim Rich that worked as an attending nurse for Marie Richmond at the hospital where she died ... guess who?" Bailey said as Jon's eyes widened at the horror of it.

"Morphine drip to the last drop, babe," Bailey added with his off colored sense of humor. Jon cringed inside. He realized that this woman would stop at nothing until she had satisfied her need for retribution against Norma and her family. He was even more frightened for Norma.

This explained everything about her strange hatred of Norma. She was out to get her from the start. All of the money and success in the world could never have filled Kim's contempt. He felt sorry for her in a way, all eaten up with bitterness and rage all of these years.

"Yeah, buddy who would have guessed? I suppose once Kim found out who her older sis was for sure, she set out to get her. She blames Norma and her mother for her mom's death. Looks like she had been planning all of this for a very long time. Boy, did she do a number on her, on everybody." Bailey held out his hand to receive his well-deserved wage. Jon paid the man and hurried out of his seat. He had to get back to the one woman who set his heart on fire.

"Try to get some rest Ms. Richmond. I promise you will feel better in the morning," the nurse said, as Norma fluttered her eyes. Her vision was blurry from the medication.

Juanita had visited earlier, and promised to bring Flora later. She had hardly been lucid. She hated being stuck here in this bed helpless and dependent. Where was Jon anyway? It had been late afternoon since she had seen him. It was sometime scary to her, how much she loved him.

Her mind meandered continuously. She was still trying to piece together the whys and hows of it all. Norma could not understand why Kim had done this. What finally tipped her over the edge? Was it Fredericko? Was she in love with him? Was losing a phony company title that important to her? Was it the money? Was Jim leaving her because of what happened?

Norma's mind wandered in and out of consciousness, as she struggled for some tangible solution. She finally surrendered her mind and thoughts to rest. She could not figure it out tonight, anyway. Norma closed her eyes and began to surrender to sweet sleep.

She was awakened several moments later by a crashing sound, and a cold breeze. "Who's there?" Norma blinked her eyes, her vision still fuzzy. Norma's eyes began to close again, heavy from all of the sedation.

About ten minutes passed, enough time for her to finally resolve her body to rest. Once again, a sound alarmed her, disturbing her, a crashing sound once more.

Her eyes settled on the window, open. She could not see clearly, but it seemed as if the window had been left open. The wind was blowing it back and forth, making a crashing sound against the frame.

"Ah, it's just the window," she sighed aloud. A nurse must have opened it. As she began to close her eyes once more, she caught a glimpse of a dark shadow out of the corner of her eye. Norma struggled to make out the image. Her eyes spread wide with sheer terror. Her heart was pounding, as she tried to call out. She was still too weak.

The shadow came closer, and then a figure emerged. Oh God, this had to be a nightmare. Norma attempted to sit up to call the nurse, her body felt as if it were weighed down by a ton of bricks. She lay there helpless, as the figure now raced towards her to cover her mouth. Norma's heart beat in sheer terror. She could see that there was something in the hand, a syringe maybe.

"You can't see me, can you? You bitch!" the voice was unmistakably Kim's.

"But I thought ..." Norma struggled for words. Kim placed a tight grip over her mouth.

"Shut-up! Or I will shoot you with enough of this to make you shut up for good! It's my turn for a spotlight. Did you really think that I wouldn't come back for you? After what you put me through? Do you think that I could possibly *let* you live?" Kim said, sounding breathless and desperate.

Norma had never been more terrified. She struggled for breath. She just knew that she would faint at any moment. She fought to hold on.

When Kim relieved her mouth Norma began, "What I did to you? What about what you have done to me?" Norma did not care anymore. If she was there to kill her, she would do it anyway.

"Shut-up! You're just trying to confuse me! You robbed me of everything. A normal life ... a family ... a father, a mother!" Kim cried now, almost breaking down.

"What the hell are you talking about? " Norma asked, puzzled by her statement.

"You, and your bitch mother. You took him away. You made him deny us. My mother cried for him everyday. I watched her die, do you know what that's like? Do you have any idea?" Kim asked rhetorically. Her voice and eyes were mad with unspeakable rage.

Kim sobbed and put her head down, as Norma struggled to reach the nurse's call button. "It's all over now," Kim said pulling out what looked like a gun.

Norma closed her eyes, and took a deep breath. Her life passed before her eyes. Here this was supposed to have been the best night of her life. Look how it was all about to end. Not here, not like this. Norma tried to make peace with her maker, asking for forgiveness and begging Him to accept her soul.

An unfamiliar voice rang out, "All right Kimberley Whaley, you are under arrest." The detective struggled with Kim for a moment. He finally knocked the gun away from her hand, getting enough of a grip to cuff her.

Jon raced to Norma's side, "Norma are you all right?" Jon said, kissing the top of her head and wiping her tears away.

Norma smiled with her eyes. There he was again, her knight in shining armor, rescuing her again. She loved him so, especially at this moment.

"Be careful ... she ... she's got something in her ..." Norma began.

"Oh, you mean this syringe she filled with water?" the detective said, snatching it and placing it on a nearby table. Jon was glad he had followed him.

"I don't think that would have hurt you, but that gun could sure do the trick. Good thing I followed you here," he addressed Jon as the hospital security and other authorities began to arrive.

"You ... left your wallet. I may overcharge, but I never rob my customers blind," he handed Jon his wallet in the restaurant. Bailey walked towards the hospital door to assist the police outside with Kim's arrest. Jon was grateful for his help, *and* his wacky sense of humor at this point.

"I can't thank you enough," he said, firmly shaking his hand before he nodded and disappeared behind the hospital door.

"Jon, oh ... I'm so glad you're here. Kim was saying some strange things. I think she's gone completely nuts. She was blaming me for being an orphan and ..." Norma began.

"Norma, Kim may very well be crazy, but I am willing to bet you that she was finally telling you the truth just now," Jon began, trying to hold the truth just another day. He wanted so to protect and love her forever. He was not sure if Norma could handle anymore right now. Enough was enough.

"Jon, what are you talking about?" Norma was now desperate for the real truth.

"Norma, baby, trust me when I tell you that it ... it can wait."

"No, Jon please tell me now," Norma insisted.

"Okay," Jon took a seat and grasped Norma's hand.

"Norma, I really don't know how to come out and say this."

"Jon just ..." Norma begged with her eyes.

"Okay ... you've been asking why Kim would do such

horrible things ... why she could hate you so much. Norma ... your father had an affair with Kim's mother years ago. Apparently, the town somehow found out about it. Everyone sort of kept it hidden for years, since your father was so well-respected," Jon swallowed hard and carefully studied Norma's reaction.

Norma turned her eyes away from Jon, as if he had betrayed her, "It's not true. My father was a decent man."

"Kim is the product of that affair. She is your half-sister," Jon said, smoothing his hand across her head to comfort her. He could see the pain surfacing in her exhausted face.

"No, I don't believe you! It can't be true. My father ..." Norma grimaced in pain.

"Norma, I saw the birth certificate with his name on it," Jon stared into Norma's eyes of disbelief.

"It could have been forged! Anything, oh Jon ... it can't be true!" Norma sobbed at the idea of such a betrayal from her father.

A dead silence fell on the room. Norma searched for some understanding. Jon gave her that time to grieve. He would withhold the part about Marie, until she was better.

Norma tried to absorb all that she had learned. Suddenly, it all began to make sense. After a few moments, Norma realized that it was truly the only thing that did make sense.

The pieces of the puzzle gathered quickly in Norma's mind now. She began to slowly recall the weird familiarity about Kim when she first met her. She remembered thinking how much alike they seemed, even down to facial expressions that only she and her sisters had shared. She had thought of her as a kindred spirit. Now, she understood why. Norma had thought it just out of friendship, a sharing of ambitions and talents.

Norma understood Kim's deep hatred of her now. Her mind held on to the angry words that Kim had spoken only moments before, "You robbed me of everything! A normal life ... a family, a father, a mother!" It all made sense now. Deep down, Kim was

Kim was still that angry little twelve year old orphan who only wanted her mother back. She had looked for love everywhere, and come up empty. As Norma peered through the opaque hospital window, she could see Kim's emotionless face, staring straight ahead at nothing. She just stood there stone faced, as the officers read her rights.

A deep sense of pity overtook Norma, as they finally carried Kim away on a hospital stretcher. And to think, it was never really about Jim at all. It was never about money, or a title, nor anything that could ever have been satisfied. She had lived and breathed for her revenge, until it had finally come to destroy her. Norma felt a deep sense of sorrow. Her heart ached for this poor tormented soul, lost, full of anger and pain, now linked to her by her own blood.

Norma then peered up at Jonathon, who was overwhelmed with the thought that again, he had almost lost her. Love shone in his marvelously brown eyes. He was so grateful that Kim would finally be brought to the justice that she deserved, no matter what her issues. His eyes were filled with tears, as he mouthed the words, "I love you."

Norma attempted to bow her head to his expected gentle kiss. She looked up and realized that he was all that she wanted right now. He had stood by her through some trying times. "I love you, too," Norma said aloud, without a second thought. Tears came streaming down her face, but there was no shame. She had never felt this way about anyone. He had proven his love and loyalty without question.

"Then be my wife," Jon said, putting one finger across her lips to silence her. "Don't answer now, just think about it. I already know you have protests," he smiled and whispered. She smiled. He knew her so well.

"Now with no further ado, there's someone who really wants to see you," Jon said stepping out of the way, and allowing Flora to step closer. Norma only wished her vision was a bit clearer, but even with her eyes blurry she could recognize Flora.

Flora stepped forward. She was a bit chubbier than Norma

had remembered, and her hair was longer. Flora was the shortest of the three of them, 5' 7". She could not make out her features clearly, but she could tell that she was smiling bright and wide. An adolescent child of about twelve held her hand tightly, as they approached Norma's bed. Norma opened her mouth in delight.

"Flora is this?" Norma began.

"Jennifer, yor' niece. She wanted tuh meet you, too," Flora said, her piercing accent as strong as her mother's had been.

Flora embraced her gently, but Norma held her tight, so happy that she was there.

"I can hardly believe you are standing there," Norma was filled with overwhelming joy. Flora rubbed her arm. They had not spoken for too long. All those years had passed. Look what she had missed, another grandchild for Marie.

"Norma, don' try tah talk, you too weak," Flora said, content to stand there and see her oldest sister. She had missed her so.

Flora saw how beautiful Norma still was, even through the ugliness of her confinement. A twinge of jealously surged through her, her own personal appearance being a challenge to maintain. Juanita and Norma had been more blessed in that area.

"But, there is so much to say," Norma struggled with words. She could only imagine what was going on inside her head. Norma sighed, frustrated at her weak condition. She could hardly even keep her eyes open. There was so much that needed to be said, so much to make amends for.

"Yes, I know. An' we gon' spend time sayin' it all. I'll be heah fo' least three weeks." Flora squeezed Norma's hand tightly.

"Three weeks?" Norma said in shock. "But what about ..."

"He said it was okay. So looks like you gon' have us in yo hair fo' a while," Flora sat in silent repose, holding her hand, not quite sure what to say after all of the time that had passed between them.

"All right, all right, break it up," Juanita finally waltzed in, after asking about a million questions to Jon and the police. "Well, heard you had enough action for a Miami Vice episode tonight."

Juanita had only left the hospital an hour after receiving Jon's worried call. She was glad that he had made it in time. Norma really had a winner this time around. Finally the ole' girl had found the right one. She only hoped Norma had enough sense not to let this one get away.

"Oh, Nita, it would be Miami Vice with you," Norma said teasingly.

"I see you've met your niece. So, next time it's your turn to come round and see us all in ole' Ginia. Listen honey, when you git outta here, we all gonna have a big slumber party and go through all your fan mail," Juanita said, chuckling at Norma's expression.

"Fan mail?" Norma asked in shock.

"Yeah girl, you can not imagine how many letters have come in. Everyone is rooting for you, love. You got about a dozen flowers, and a Michelle Windom came by to drop off your award," Juanita glowed with pride for her sister.

"Oh, it's so good to have you all here. I thought that my best moment would have come on that stage last night. But turns out its here with the two ... I mean the three of you," Norma smiled at her niece.

"Oh shucks, Norma stop being so corny, girl. Besides, where you expect us to be. We's yah sistas," Nita said, as they all chuckled away.

"How's that baby boy you got, sis?" Norma remembered that Juanita was quite pregnant the last time she came for a visit. She looked good, all considered.

"Just fine, honey girl ... just crawlin' around. His daddy is so proud, yah know." Jon and the nurse entered the room.

"Well ladies, sorry to break up the party, but I think someone had better get some rest tonight," Jon said as Norma frowned.

"Oh no Jon ... it was just getting fun in here," Norma began. Flora and Juanita said their good-byes for the evening. Jon was right. It had been quite an evening, and she had never rested completely.

180

"Hey, think about what I said when you get a chance," Jon whispered softly and kissed her before she could say anything.

"But ..." Norma began, but he had already disappeared behind the door. He knew her all too well. Sure she had protests. There were so many things to consider. It did not mean that she was not in love with him. She just needed a little more time.

Norma's mind and body were exhausted from the day's adventures. Norma decided to let go of it all for tonight. She closed her eyes, surrendering to the sweetest dreams.

Chapter
<u>16</u>

New Beginnings

"We find the defendant Kimberley Whaley guilty on two counts of attempted murder," the foreman declared. The courtroom full of Ecstacy staff and models cheered on. Jonathon and Norma embraced as the verdict was rendered.

"Order!" the judge shouted, "Mrs. Whaley, do you have anything that you would like to say?"

Kim stood up slowly. A hush fell over the courtroom, as everyone sat in anticipation of her words. Kim finally turned directly towards Norma and yelled uncontrollably, "I hope you are satisfied! You both destroyed my mother! Now, you have destroyed me!" She advanced towards Norma, but her defense team held her back. The courtroom was in an uproar.

Norma shook her head, as the judge attempted to gain control over his courtroom.

"Order! Order! Order!" he yelled, the chaos finally dying down.

"Due to the malicious nature of the crimes committed, the court sentences the defendant to no less than a twenty-five year sentence in a women's correctional facility without the possibility of parole. Bailiff, please remove the defendant from this courtroom and remand her into custody immediately," the judge proclaimed with eyes of steel. He felt that justice had been served well in this particular case.

Kim cried and screamed I hate yous' in Norma's direction all the way out the door, handcuffs and all. Norma placed her head in her hands, shaking her head from side to side. Kim's rage had taken what was left of her mind. Jon consoled Norma by rubbing her back.

"This court is adjourned!" the judge finally declared. Everyone sighed relief. Now, it was finally over.

It had been a long nine months in the system, three of which Kim vehemently denied her guilt. She showed no sign of remorse for anything, but continued to blame Norma at every given opportunity.

Jim had made several appearances in the courtroom, his head down to Norma. Norma had not seen him for several months now. Norma understood his embarrassment, and avoided any confrontation when she did see him. Besides, she could not blame Jim for Kim's hatred.

In the meantime, Jon and Norma had continued to get closer in *every* way. Jon was as gentle and wonderful a lover as he had been a friend and confidant. He made love to her with such passion, and true, sincere love. She had never been more satisfied.

Norma smiled to herself, right there in the courtroom, as she recalled the night that their passion was finally made complete. It was after an especially trying day in court. Instead of going out to dinner that night, they had decided to order in and watch movies at Jon's place.

That night had been no different than most. They had talked, laughed, and relished every moment of time together. After all of the conversation and movies were complete, Jon amorously touched her lips with his. Norma surprised him by not only welcoming his kisses, but entwining her tongue with his. She began undressing him as well.

Jon smoothed his hands gently over her beautiful shiny hair, which was hanging freely to her shoulders that evening. He had waited so long for this moment. His only desire was to cherish every part of her gorgeous anatomy, make her feel beautiful all over. He wanted to engulf her in the waves of his igniting passion.

Jon succulently kissed and tasted her, beginning with her hands, working his way to her arms, her neck, her chests, and finally ... slowly ... tastefully ... her breasts. He stayed there for what seemed an eternity, biting, touching, and kissing, until Norma could no longer hold in her cries of fervent passion.

Jon smiled at the look of erotic euphoria on her face, then decided to venture on to other parts of her anxious body. He aroused her even more as he explored wet, erogenous zones, taking her into realms of erotic love where she had never ever dare gone before.

His manhood finally entered her, as his rhythm drummed with impeccable grace and timeliness. Jon was such a spectacular lover, stroking her with the genius and expertise of ageless lovers of the triumphant past. They moaned together, no inhibitions between them, finally climaxing in unison.

Norma had sat staring into space in the after glow of love, staring at the moonlit sky from Jon's bed. She had peered over at Jon, afraid that it had all been a dream. Jon had loved her body as no man had. He had touched every part of her with care, love, and genuine understanding. His love satisfied not only her body, but her very soul. He was her mate in every way imaginable, and lovemaking was no exception.

He had never pressured her about his proposal, as they continued to enjoy one another. The more she got to know Jon, the more she wanted and loved him. Her sister told her that she was crazy for not saying yes, while constantly reminding her of her age. "You know girl, yah ain't gettin' no younger," Juanita would say.

Norma could not be rushed. Norma's heart was still aching a little from making bad decisions in love. She had loved Jim with all of her heart, and he had only broken it. She wanted to make sure that this was the real thing, once and for all.

Norma blinked into reality, finally realizing where she was again She looked around to see that almost everyone had gone. Jon noticed the far away look in her eye, and wondered where her mind had been.

"Norma, sweetheart, are you all right?" Jon said, looking a bit puzzled.

Norma and Jon gathered their things to leave the courtroom, as a thin man dressed in a suit approached them. Norma squinted her eyes as if that could make her better recognize this stranger. As he approached her, Norma finally recognized him. She pulled her head back in shock.

"Norma I am so so sorry," a familiar but weak voice said extending his hand.

"Jim!" Norma said, embarrassed that she had not recognized her own ex-husband.

"Norma do you want me to ..." Jon began. He would not allow her to be hurt by him anymore.

"Jonathon, can I meet you outside?" Norma asked with her mouth and her eyes. Jon relented, but was quite unhappy about it.

"Sure," he said, kissing her on the cheek, but with little heart. He had only wanted to protect her. This lady had a heart of gold. That bastard had put her through so much. He would always protect her now.

Jon left, as Jim smiled watching him leave.

"You found someone worthy of your love," Jim said coughing. It was apparent that he was sick. She wondered if his years of philandering had finally caught up with him.

"I know what you are thinking, but it's not that. I do not have Aids. Worse. It's liver sclerosis. The doctors say there is a good chance to beat this thing. I definitely had to stop drinking ... but it's still not easy," Jim shook his head and turned his eyes away.

"Oh Jim, I am so sorry ...." Norma said cautiously. Jim had always been a man of pride. His looks had been his calling card.

This emaciated Jim was not the one she had known. She was not sure what else she could say.

"No, it's me that's sorry. I had to come and say that Norma Jeanette. I took advantage of a beautiful, smart, and sweet lady once. Now look at what card I got dealt. And Kim, oh God ... Kim ..." he stopped for a moment, putting his face in his hands and weeping.

"You really loved her, didn't you?" Norma asked, feeling a small lump in her throat. Jim nodded, yes. That hurt like hell, for Kim had loved no one. She had only used others as pawns in her evil plot.

"Anyway, I had to say I was sorry for everything. I thought you could get some sort of satisfaction."

"What, to see you like this? No, how could you think that about me? Don't you know me better than that?" Norma did not know whether she pitied him or Kim more now.

"Yeah, I guess I should. You are one helluva lady Norma Richmond, and I am proud to say that you were once my wife," he said, embracing Norma.

"I forgive you and I release you," Norma thought to herself, as they embraced. A new peace overtook her. A burden seemed lifted off of her shoulders. She realized that this whole ordeal was finally over once and for all. It had finally come full circle, and been resolved.

"Thank you, Jim," Norma said catching a glance of a very red-faced jealous man out of the corner of her eye. "Thank you, but I have to go," she tilted her head. Jim watched Jon rushing way. Jim nodded with understanding, as Norma tried to catch up to an angry Jonathon, now heading towards his car at top speed.

"Newman!" Norma yelled, after she was tired of running after him.

Jon stopped in surprise. He had never heard her address him by his last name, especially not since they had started dating.

"What?" he answered in a harsh tone, but stopped dead in his tracks.

Norma smiled. He stopped exactly as she had wanted him to, giving her just enough time to catch up.

"Jon, wait up," Norma was finally close enough to reach out for his hand.

Jon rejected her hand, but turned to face her, his face red with jealousy, his eyes filled with love. "You can't imagine how it makes me feel to see that jerk touching you," Jon held out his hands, clawing his fingers at the air and gritting his lips in utter frustration. Norma had never seen him like this before. Jon had always been so cool and suave. Norma contemplated her next move.

"But Jon, baby I needed to make amends. Don't you see that? Jon, I could never want Jim again ... *I Love You*," Norma gazed directly into his beautiful brown eyes, all brazen with hurt and frustration.

"Well ... just ... I ... I ... need to think ... call me later," he said, turning to walk away from her again.

Call him later, what? This was not going the way she had planned. She could not just let him walk away mad, not like this. Jim would not ruin her good thing once again. Norma wanted Jon to know that he had 100% of her love, forever.

"Hey ... I was just wondering if I was going to leave the Richmond in my name after Newman," Norma began nonchalantly.

"What?" Jon said, stopping in front of his car door and turning to face her once again.

"I mean, Norma Newman sounds dumb all by itself. What do you think?" she said, getting close enough to hold on to his arm tightly.

Jon could no longer be angry. He shook his head at her and began smiling a bit. "Are you saying what I think you...."

"Yes!" Norma exclaimed. Jon picked her up to swing in the air. That was no easy feat. Norma was a strong, tall woman.

"Yes, Mr. Jonathon Newman, I will be your wife," Norma said smiling and crying all at the same time. She had never been happier, nor more certain of any one thing. Jon kissed her passionately, and they embraced. Norma looked up smiling, sure that Mama was watching from heaven and thought, "Now *this* Mama, is *Ecstasy.*"

Ecstacy

Norma Jeanette Richmond had it all. She was a beautiful, intelligent, and a successful Black woman. She made her success as a model on the streets of New York, and then went on to build her own modeling agency, Ecstacy Enterprises. Ecstacy Enterprises was on the cutting edge of the modeling industry with two branches located in New York, Los Angeles, and one soon to be in Oakland or San Francisco. Then, Norma met Jim Whaley and Kimberley Brandon, two people who changed her life forever. After a string of hard times and heartaches, Norma finds faith again to rise above her struggles to reach the highest state of her own true ecstasy.

BOOK AVAILABLE THROUGH
Milligan Books, Inc.
An Imprint of Professional Business Consulting Service
Ecstacy $14.95

Order Form
Milligan Books, Inc.
1425 W. Manchester Ave., Suite C, Los Angeles, CA 90047
(323) 750-3592

Name_____ Date _____

Address _____

City_____ State____ Zip Code _____

Day Telephone _____

Evening Telephone_____

Book Title_____

Number of books ordered___ Total ....$ _____

Sales Taxes (CA Add 8.25%) ....$ _____

Shipping & Handling $4.90 for one book..$ _____

Add $1.00 for each additional book..........$ _____

Total Amount Due....................................$ _____

□ Check   □ Money Order □ Other Cards _____

□ Visa   □ MasterCard Expiration Date _____

Credit Card No. _____

Driver License No. _____

Make check payable to Milligan Books, Inc.

_____   _____
Signature   Date